D1503003

Hey, TodaysGirls! Check out 2day's kewlest music, books, and stuff when u hit *spiritgirl.com*

Copyright © 2001 by Terry K. Brown

Published in Nashville, Tennessee, by Tommy Nelson®, a division of Thomas Nelson, Inc.

Scripture quotations are from the *International Children's Bible®, New Century Version®*: Copyright © 1986, 1988, 1999 by Tommy Nelson®, a division of Thomas Nelson, Inc.

Creative director: Robin Crouch
Storyline development & series continuity: Dandi Daley Mackall
Computer programming consultant: Lucinda C. Thurman

Library of Congress Cataloging-in-Publication Data

Brown, Terry, 1961-
    Fun e-Farm / created by Terry Brown.
      p. cm. – (TodaysGirls.com ; 12)
    Summary: After rescuing a litter of abandoned kittens from a dumpster, Morgan finds herself setting up an emergency animal shelter in her family's barn, without her parents' knowledge.
    ISBN 0-8499-7715-0
    [1. Animals—Treatment—Fiction. 2. Christian life—Fiction.] I. Title. II. Series.

PZ7.B8178 Fu 2001
[Fic]—dc21   2001030543

Printed in the United States of America

01 02 03 04 05 PHX 9 8 7 6 5 4 3 2 1

FUN e-FARM

WRITTEN BY
Heather Wiseman

CREATED BY
Terry K. Brown

Thomas Nelson, Inc. • Nashville

YA
WIS

Web Words

2 to/too

4 for

ACK! disgusted

AIMP always in my prayers

A/S/L age/sex/location

B4 before

BBL be back later

BBS be back soon

BD big deal

BF boyfriend

BFN bye for now

BRB be right back

BTW by the way

CU see you

Cuz because

CYAL8R see you later

Dunno don't know

Enuf enough

FWIW for what it's worth

FYI for your information

G2G or **GTG** I've got to go

GF girlfriend

GR8 great

H&K hug and kiss

IC I see

IN2 into

IRL in real life

JK just kidding

JLY Jesus loves you

JMO just my opinion

K okay

Kewl cool

KOTC kiss on the cheek

L8R later

LOL laugh out loud

LTNC long time no see

LY love you

NBD no big deal

NU new/knew

NW no way

OIC oh, I see

QT cutie

RO rock on

ROFL rolling on floor laughing

RU are you

SOL sooner or later

Splain explain

SWAK sealed with a kiss

SYS see you soon

Thanx (or) **thx** thanks

TNT till next time

TTFN ta ta for now

TTYL talk to you later

U you

U NO you know

UD you'd (you would)

UR your/you're/you are

WB welcome back

WBS write back soon

WTG way to go

Y why

(Note: Remember that capitalization may vary.)

chapter.1

Can't you move any faster?" Maya snapped.

"It's only ten after nine." Morgan glanced at her older sister and continued wiping the booth by the restaurant window. "There's nothing to do on a Monday night anyway."

"Just because *you* don't have a life this summer, don't assume no one else does." Maya overturned chairs on the tables to clear the floor for sweeping. "Now get your rear in gear. I can't leave till everything's clean."

"Got a hot date?"

"Bren and I are hitting the mall's Midnight Madness sale. All the stores stay open late, and at midnight they slash prices on everything!"

"You call that having a life?"

"Girls, girls!" their mom said, coming through the restaurant's swinging kitchen door. "Stop sniping at each other."

Morgan wiped the last booth and grabbed her plastic tub of dirty dishes. "Where's Dad?"

"Back in the office." Her mom opened the cash register and removed stacks of bills to count.

Morgan headed toward the kitchen of their fifties-style diner, the Gnosh Pit. With its walls decorated with old car parts and fake neon signs, the Gnosh was a local teen hangout on nights and weekends, while it served a regular group of adults for breakfast and lunch. The kitchen was like an oven, Morgan thought as she stacked dirty dishes into the dishwasher.

"How's it going?" she asked Jamie, who was scouring the griddle.

"Nearly done." Jamie worked part-time and was one of Morgan and Maya's closest friends. "Benny's a great cook, but what a slob! There's grease splattered everywhere. I hate when the special's fried fish."

Morgan rinsed the plastic tub. "Wish we were at the pool right now." She glanced at the water-stained wall calendar over the sink. She couldn't believe the summer was half over already.

"Me too." Jamie wiped the perspiration from her upper lip. "I'll be online later to chat though, in case anyone's around. I'm glad we changed summer chat to ten o'clock."

Morgan filled a wicker basket with salt, sugar packets, and rolls of mints to replenish the tables and restock the glass case.

Just then the phone rang. As it rang a second time, Jamie reached for it. Morgan shook her head. "Dad's in the office. He'll get it."

Morgan stepped out the back door for a moment, hoping to catch some breeze. The kitchen was stifling, in spite of air conditioning and the ceiling fan. When she came back inside, she heard raised voices out in the dining room. Her mom sounded worried, but Morgan couldn't make out the words. Grabbing the wicker basket, she hurried from the kitchen.

Her parents and Maya were standing at the cash register. "I can't believe it," her mom said. "The poor thing. I never knew she was sick."

Mr. Cross hugged his wife close. "From what Rose said, it was very sudden."

"Edith was always frail," Mrs. Cross said, "ever since Walter died. Rose gave up her job to move into that old monstrosity of a house to take care of her."

"What's going on?" Morgan asked.

Her mom turned. "I just got some bad news. My aunt Rose called from Johnston. Apparently Aunt Edith passed away suddenly this morning."

"I'm sorry." Morgan frowned. "Was Aunt Edith the older one?"

"Yes, mid-seventies, I think. Rose is just in her early sixties. She never married, and she moved in with Edith after her husband died." Mrs. Cross rubbed her forehead. "Now she needs my help to sort through things and sell the house."

Maya stopped sweeping and leaned on her broom. "Why do you have to go help? Can't someone else do it?"

"I live the closest, even though Johnston's six hours away. Plus I'm not teaching summer school, so I'm free to go. But what a huge job!" She rested her head briefly on her husband's shoulder. "I could really use some help."

Morgan leaned on the counter. "How long will you be gone?"

"I'll go right away to help with funeral arrangements, but sorting through things and helping Rose find a place to live could take a week. Maybe even two."

"You know I'd come if I could," her husband said.

"I know. But then, who'd run the restaurant?" Mrs. Cross straightened, then turned to Maya. "On the other hand . . ."

Maya stuck out one hand like a traffic cop. "Hey, I can't go! I've got too much to do myself."

Her mom sighed, and Morgan gave her a hug. "I'm sorry, Mom. Did you really like Aunt Edith?"

"To be honest, I didn't know her that well. I didn't keep in touch like I should have. I was always closer to Rose." She grinned suddenly. "Edith was cranky, but Aunt Rose knew how to have fun with kids. Since I was an only child, I loved when she made time to play with me. The least I can do now is be there for her."

"When will you leave?" Morgan asked.

"First thing in the morning. Before six probably. In fact, I'd better get home now and pack."

4

"I'll drive you there," Mr. Cross said. "I want to check the oil and washer fluid in the van before you take off." He turned to Maya. "You girls finish up, okay? We'll see you at home."

As soon as their parents walked out the front door, Maya said, "Move your carcass. I've got places to go and things to do."

Rolling her eyes, Morgan returned to the kitchen to finish her shift. Jamie was done with the griddle and already sweeping the tile floor. "There's just the garbage left," she said.

Morgan wrinkled her nose. She hated going out back to the Dumpster. Oh well, at least it wasn't winter and cold and dark. On the other hand, nothing stank worse than a Dumpster full of rotten food on a sweltering summer day.

Sighing, Morgan bagged up the trash and stacked it by the back door. Then, grabbing two black bags in each hand, she dragged them outside to the green metal Dumpster. As she raised the heavy plastic lid and tossed in the first bag, something in the Dumpster squeaked and squealed. Morgan screamed, dropped the lid, and raced back inside the Gnosh.

"What's the matter?" Jamie asked, meeting her at the kitchen door.

"I—I—I don't know." Sheepishly, Morgan pointed. "There's something *alive* in there!"

Jamie laughed. "You probably surprised a raccoon or squirrel. Come on."

Feeling foolish, Morgan caught her breath. "It's okay. I can do it."

But Jamie went with her and carefully lifted the Dumpster lid. "Hey, I hear something too."

Morgan inched closer and listened. Something—or several somethings—were squealing. Her eyes opened wide. "Kittens!"

Morgan leaned over the side of the Dumpster, ignoring the horrid fumes of hot rotten garbage as she sorted among the bags and boxes. With her head in the Dumpster, she could tell the mewing sounds came from a bag in the far corner.

"There's a burlap bag over there." Morgan stretched, but it was just out of her reach. She jumped up and teetered precariously on the edge of the Dumpster, balancing on her stomach. "Grab my legs so I don't fall in."

Jamie gripped her around the knees while Morgan stretched as far as she could. Her fingers were just a couple of inches short of reaching the burlap bag. The mewing and squealing grew louder. Morgan rocked from side to side to wiggle herself forward. And banged her right hipbone hard on the metal edge of the Dumpster.

"Owww!"

She jerked forward off her hipbones, kicking Jamie's head in the process. "Hey!" Jamie yelled, letting go.

Morgan went face first into the Dumpster, landing in a cardboard box of rotten bananas and tomatoes. She scraped her legs when she fell in, and the squealing doubled in volume.

"Help!" she cried, trying to get her footing while wiping squished tomatoes from her face and neck.

"I'm sorry!" Jamie reached to help her friend. "Grab my hand."

But as Morgan stood there, knee-deep in black plastic garbage bags, boxes of wilted lettuce, and half-eaten cantaloupes, the squealing quieted. Morgan leaned over and grasped the knotted end of the burlap bag and pulled. It was heavy. Dragging it closer, she lifted it up to Jamie, then jumped up on the Dumpster's edge, swung her leg over, and dropped to the ground. Jamie quickly tossed in the other Gnosh garbage and closed the lid.

Morgan dropped to her knees on the gravel and pulled on the twisted knot of the bag. Tiny bumps and bulges appeared and disappeared against the bag's sides. Finally she got the bag untied and peered inside.

"Look!" Morgan held the bag open for Jamie. "There are four—no *five*—kittens in here! Someone threw them away! They would have suffocated—or starved to death!"

"Or been crushed when the Dumpster got emptied," Jamie added.

Morgan shivered. "What if I hadn't come out here tonight and heard them? What if they'd—"

"But you did," Jamie interrupted. "Now what?"

"I'll take them home! What else?" But when she carried the mewing bag of kittens back into the Gnosh, Maya had other ideas.

"You're *what*?" Maya said. "Like I don't think so!"

"Mom and Dad will let me keep them."

"Are your brains totally fried? They will not."

"They let us keep Vinnie when we found him."

"That was only one cat. And he only hung around a month before running off again." Maya peered into the bag. "You've got five! No way can you keep them. They're filthy and so are you!"

Morgan reached into the bag and lifted out two gold tiger kittens. "Here," she said, handing them to Jamie.

She reached in again and lifted out another kitten, this one much smaller than the others, all black and white with a black mask around its eyes. "Ohhh! Look!" Morgan held him out. "He looks like Zorro!"

Jamie snuggled the tiger kittens close in her apron. "What will you do with them then?" she asked.

"Could you take them home just for tonight?"

"I wish I could. We really don't have the room. Anyway, my sisters would get attached, then have a fit when they couldn't keep them."

"Then I'll just have to take them home," Morgan said, washing her face and neck and hands at the sink. "Mom and Dad'll understand. I'll keep them in our barn. It's empty."

"Dream on, turkey," Maya said.

"You have a barn?" Jamie's eyes opened wide. "Where? I've never seen it."

"It's way at the back of our five acres," Maya said, "behind that row of tall trees."

"A barn in town?"

"Our place used to be *outside* Edgewood," Maya explained, "back when it was a farm, with animals and everything. Mom inherited the acreage from her parents."

"Yeah," Morgan added as she warmed a pan of milk. "Around World War II or something Grandpa sold off his land when the town grew out that way."

Maya nodded. "He kept five acres and the barn, but Mom said they knocked down the old farmhouse when they built our brick one."

Soon the five kittens were lapping warm milk from two pie pans. Zorro kept sticking his nose in too far, then sneezing milk. He licked the milk droplets from his whiskers.

"Should I heat some more milk?" Morgan asked after they emptied the pans.

Jamie touched the bulging sides of the kittens. "Better not. They might pop. Their little tummies are hard as rocks."

Maya jingled her car keys. "Hurry it up. At this rate I'll miss the Midnight Madness sale."

Morgan wiped her legs with paper towels while Jamie found a cardboard box in the storage room for the kittens so they wouldn't be bunched together in the bag. Morgan slid the box into the backseat of Mr. Beep, the old Volkswagen Beetle Maya had inherited from her mom's college days.

First they dropped Jamie off. "Can I leave the box in here when we get home?" Morgan asked, peering over the backseat. "Please? Just till I can talk to Mom and Dad?"

"Well . . . I guess so, but get real. You know you can't keep them."

Morgan didn't reply as they pulled onto Jackson Street. Maya turned in at their two-story home, then parked behind her dad's vintage car. Morgan took a deep breath. Her parents just *had* to let her keep those abandoned kittens. Somehow she'd find a way to convince them.

But when they went inside, there was no chance for Morgan to talk to her parents about the kittens. Their mom was writing lists, sticking them to the refrigerator with magnets. Dad was hauling suitcases up from the basement.

Maya eyed them suspiciously. "Why so many bags? Are you staying a month?"

"No, honey. I'm not." Mrs. Cross moved around the breakfast bar to unload the dishwasher. "Actually, half those suitcases are for you."

"Oh no, they aren't!" Maya backed up so fast she knocked their blue see-through phone from the counter to the floor.

"I'm afraid it's necessary, Maya, and I wish you'd adjust your attitude." Mrs. Cross picked up the phone. "This isn't fun for me either." She took a deep breath. "Aunt Rose doesn't want to live alone in that huge old house, and I don't blame her. It has to be cleaned and sold. So I need your help."

"But I can't! The mall just got in the fall clothes, and I've got a date this weekend."

Her mom turned from where she was putting glasses in the

cupboard. "You'll pardon me if I don't find that earth-shaking at a time like this."

"Why can't Morgan go? She never does anything important!"

"Thanks a lot," Morgan said.

"Well, you don't."

"Stop it, girls." Mrs. Cross sorted silverware into the drawer. "Maya, I need you to go because you have a driver's license. You can help with moving and running errands."

"But—but—what about my job?" She turned to her dad. "You can't spare me. Can you, Dad? I don't want to leave you short-handed."

"I can manage. Actually, I already called Amber to see if she could put in some hours for a couple weeks due to our family emergency. She was more than happy to help." He glanced at Morgan. "I'm sure I can count on your sister if I need an extra set of hands."

"No problem," Morgan said.

"Traitor!" Maya snapped.

"That's enough." Mr. Cross put an arm around his wife. "Stop thinking of yourself for one minute and give some thought to helping your mom."

"But I don't want to hang out with some old lady cleaning a haunted house. Somebody just *died* there!"

"That's *enough*." He handed her two small suitcases. "You'll leave first thing in the morning, so you'd better go pack."

"I don't believe this!" Maya grabbed the bags and stomped

out of the kitchen. Morgan held her breath till she heard Maya's bedroom door slam.

"Well, wasn't that fun?" Her dad laughed. "Don't worry, honey. She'll come around and be a good help to you."

"I know."

Morgan hugged her mom, but she didn't have half the faith in Maya that her parents did. When Maya didn't get her way, she could be a mega monster to live with.

chapter.2

Morgan glanced at the microwave clock and saw it was nearly ten already. She wished she could join the TodaysGirls chat on the big computer in Maya's room, but Morgan had no intention of walking into a grizzly bear's den right then. Why issue an open invitation to get her head bitten off?

After her parents went upstairs, Morgan opened her laptop and plugged it into the family phone line. She had permission to tie it up for just half an hour during the chat time. That way she could chat, too, while Maya was upstairs on their line.

When Morgan logged on to TodaysGirls.com, the familiar magenta screen loaded. When it finished, she entered her password, and Amber's Thought for the Day popped open. Morgan clicked it closed without reading it, then clicked into the chat room. Jamie, Amber, Alex, and Bren were already there. Hmm, her sister hadn't logged on yet. Should she remind her what time it was? No, Morgan decided, Maya'd called her a traitor. She'd better lie low.

Settling down on the bar stool, Morgan thought about how each girl's screen name fit her so well. Alex from Texas was TX2step, artistic Jamie was rembrandt, Bren the shopper was chicChick. Amber seemed to have the whole Bible memorized—she was faithful1. And Morgan herself was jellybean, her dad's pet name for her since she was a baby.

> **chicChick:** well, the Cross girls join us.
>
> **faithful1:** 1 of them. where's Maya?
>
> **jellybean:** upstairs packing. MAD. she has to go with mom tomorrow.
>
> **TX2step:** where?
>
> **jellybean:** Johnston. mom's aunt died and her other aunt needs help moving. Maya has to go help pack and clean and stuff.
>
> **chicChick:** what about shopping tonite? she's picking me up! where R her priorities?
>
> **faithful1:** sorry about your aunt.
>
> **rembrandt:** I told every1 about the kittens B4 u got here. where R they?
>
> **jellybean:** asleep in the car. I'll ask about keeping them when I log off.
>
> **chicChick:** ugh. kittens r cute, but u have 2 have a stinky

litter box and 1 of those pooper scooper things

TX2step: U could just pay someone to do it 4 U

jellybean: NBD Anyway, they're so cute! The runt has a
black mask like Zorro

rembrandt: I asked 2 keep 1, but mom said there's
hardly anyone at home and it would get lonely here

chicChick: they like SHED their fur, u no! I don't care
how cute they R. Who wants cat hair on UR clothes!
and Y can't Maya take me 2 the mall if she's not leaving til tomorrow?

jellybean: wish me luck

Morgan logged off ten minutes later, then hunted in the cupboard for more crispy M&M's. Rats. They were gone. Just then
she heard her parents coming downstairs. It was now or never.
Taking a deep breath, she went looking for them. She found her
mom in the den.

"Done chatting already?" her mom asked.

"Yeah. I was wondering—" Morgan stopped. "What's with
the picture albums?"

"Rose asked if I had any good photos of Edith. She wants them
for the memorial service." She flipped several pages, then pointed.
"Here's one." She pulled the photo from under its plastic cover.

"That's Aunt Edith?"

"Yes, taken five or six years ago, after Uncle Walter died. She
was probably in her early seventies then."

Morgan bent over the photo. Aunt Edith had been a scrawny woman. Knobby knuckles protruded from the raw-looking hand that gripped her cane. Her gray hair, curled into stiff ringlets, was held in place by a hair net that came down to the center of her forehead.

"This the best picture you have?" Morgan asked dubiously.

"It *is* grim looking," her mom admitted. "I don't have any others of her alone though. Just this other one of her and Walter on their fortieth anniversary."

"Does Rose look like Edith?"

"Not at all. You wouldn't guess they were sisters."

Just then Maya flounced into the room, her hair wet from the shower. "I'm taking the laptop with me," she announced. "I refuse to be cut off from civilization while I'm gone." She came farther into the den. "Who's that?" she asked, leaning over the photo.

"That *was* Aunt Edith," her mom said.

"Oh man, look at that hair net!" Maya rolled her eyes. "Straight off a funny farm."

"Maya! How rude!"

"Funny farm?" Morgan asked. "What's that?"

Her mom glared at Maya. "A nasty name for a mental insti- tution."

"Sor-*ry*," Maya muttered.

Morgan pressed her lips together, wondering how to change the subject and ask about the kittens. "Um, before you go to bed, can I ask you and Dad something? It's a big favor, but it's really important."

"Sure, honey. What's up?"

"Where's Dad?" They heard the front door open and close.

"There he is now. He was checking the oil and getting my van ready for the trip."

Morgan froze. Her dad had been outside working on the van *parked right beside Maya's car?* Hopefully the kittens had stayed asleep and not made a sound.

Her dad walked into the den a moment later, holding Zorro in the crook of his arm.

"Where'd you find that?" Mrs. Cross said. "What a cute little guy!"

"What do you girls know about this?" he asked.

"It's what I wanted to ask you," Morgan said. "When I took out the trash at the Gnosh, I found a burlap bag full of kittens inside the Dumpster."

"Oh no!" her mom said. "How many?"

"Five. This one's the runt of the litter." Morgan took him and cradled him close. "I had to bring them home. This is Zorro. Can I keep them?"

"Five kittens?" Her mom frowned. "Oh, honey, I don't think so."

"Oh, please. I can keep them in the barn out back and work more hours at the Gnosh to pay for their food."

"Sorry, Jellybean, but there are just too many of them." Mr.

Cross shook his head. "We'll take them to the animal shelter first thing in the morning."

"But Dad!"

"Morgan, I'm really sorry."

Her mom put an arm around her shoulders. "I know you love animals, honey, but we can't save every animal in town. They're at a cute age. They'll find homes in no time."

Morgan didn't say anything but cuddled the purring kitten closer. Zorro stared at her with such innocent eyes that Morgan felt like a traitor. *If only . . .*

chapter.3

Tuesday morning, Maya and Mrs. Cross left town just after sunrise, hoping to arrive in Johnston by noon. Maya was still grumbling when they walked out the door.

"I need to get to work early this morning," said Morgan's dad as he stood with her, waving till the van turned the corner. "With Maya and your mom gone, I'll have to spend extra hours at work. I've enjoyed having your mom there during her summer break."

"Isn't Benny cooking this morning?"

"Yes, but I'll need to take your mom's spot at the cash register during the breakfast rush, so I'm going in early to do bookwork in the office first."

"Do you need me?"

"Not yet. Amber's coming in early and working all day. Jamie wants more hours too." He squeezed her shoulders. "Anytime you want to help clean at closing would be great."

"Just say the word."

They walked back toward the garage. "By the way, Amber agreed to take you and the kittens to the shelter this morning before work. She'll be here in about an hour."

"Oh." Morgan's shoulders slumped. "Okay."

"I know it's hard. I'm sorry I can't take you myself." Her dad hugged her, then jumped into his '55 Chevy parked in the garage. "I'm off. Have a good day!"

Morgan waved halfheartedly, then trudged through the garage into the utility room. She squatted down by the cardboard box of kittens. Their water dish was empty, and the bits of ham were gone, and they mewed and crawled over each other. She lifted the box to take it into the kitchen, but the bottom was wet. Ugh. She set it back down and moved the soft towel she'd laid in the bottom. It was soaked. Apparently the kittens had dumped most of the water. She couldn't take them to the shelter in that soggy box.

When she couldn't find another box in the basement or garage, Morgan slipped on her tennis shoes and headed out to the backyard. Their five acres stretched beyond the raised flower beds and cherry trees to a row of evergreen windbreak trees that separated the barn from the house. Surely there would be a box or crate in the barn she could use.

On the way to the barn Morgan glanced over at their old

playhouse, then detoured toward it. Shaped like a miniature house, with a front door and two tiny windows, the playhouse had been Morgan's favorite place to play, or just be alone, all through grade school. The front door was stuck, but she budged it open with her shoulder and, ducking her head, stepped inside. The tiny red table and chairs, the folding cot and scratchy blanket, even the chipped tea set were still there. A quick look, though, told her there was nothing to haul the kittens in. She backed out and pulled the door closed.

Behind the thick row of evergreens stood the barn, and as she approached it, Morgan wondered why she didn't get back there more often. How she'd loved playing there when she was younger! Bracing her shoulder against the rough barn door, she pushed and shoved till the big door slid open.

Inside it was already warm, despite the early morning hour and the shade from the surrounding trees. She flipped on the overhead light, but the dim bulb was little help. Squinting, Morgan peered into the shadows. She sneezed violently at the dust she stirred up.

To her left she saw one big stall and three smaller ones where her grandpa had kept horses. That's what her mom said anyway. Morgan leaned over the first stall door. Inside, an old harness hung on a couple of rusty nails, and a cracked leather saddle rode a sawhorse. Morgan recalled dragging the saddle onto a hay bale and spending many happy hours "riding" her imaginary pony.

In the center of the barn were some old gardening tools of her dad's, some twine and ropes coiled on an overturned barrel, and a roll of wire fencing. Her dad called it chicken wire, but he put it around the back edge of the vegetable garden to keep rabbits away. In the little room on the right, though, under the hayloft, Morgan found what she needed. A wooden crate, covered with cobwebs, sat in her old red wagon. She dumped out her collection of rocks and pine cones, then took the crate back to the house.

When Amber arrived, Morgan was waiting outside with the crate of kittens. She lifted them into the car, then they headed to the Have-a-Hart Animal Shelter on the west side of Edgewood. It was privately owned, and the only shelter in town.

"I hate taking the kittens there." Morgan held Zorro in her lap, while the others mewed from the crate in the backseat. "I could take care of them myself."

Amber smiled. "You want to take care of every animal in the world," she said. "How many groups do you belong to now? Save the Seals? Save the Dolphins? Save the—"

"I know, but somebody has to care!"

"I'm just teasing. I'm sorry." Amber turned onto the main drag through town. "It just seems like you're taking on too many worries. Have you prayed about it?"

"Prayed about it?" Morgan turned sideways. "What's there to pray about?"

"Help for the whole situation. God cares about the animals too. After all, he created them."

"I suppose." Morgan didn't want to argue, but she couldn't imagine bothering God for something as minor as stray kittens. Like he didn't have bigger things in the world to worry about!

They were silent until they pulled into the shelter's small parking lot and stopped beside a wooden sign with a big red heart painted on it. According to the posted hours, the shelter had opened twenty minutes ago. Morgan heard a dog barking in the distance.

"Let's do this. It won't get easier," Amber said, "and I told your dad I'd get to work early."

"Okay." Morgan nestled Zorro back in the crate with his brothers and sisters, then carried the wooden box to the front door. The closer she got to the building, the louder the barking grew.

Inside the small waiting room, Morgan set the crate down and gazed around. Shelves on two walls held a variety of pet products. No one was behind the counter. The phone rang. A teenage boy in baggy jeans and a green T-shirt rushed in just as the answering machine picked up.

"Oh! Hey," he said, looking flustered. "I didn't know anyone was here."

"I just walked in." Morgan frowned, wondering why the boy looked familiar. "I brought some kittens."

The young man, barely taller than Morgan, looked at her— sort of—but didn't meet her eyes. "Are they yours?" he asked.

Morgan had the weird feeling that he was talking to someone

behind her left ear. "No, I found them in a Dumpster last night. They're beautiful though." She reached down and picked up Zorro.

"Todd! Hurry up!" a woman's voice echoed from beyond the closed door.

"Coming!" He ducked his head in embarrassment, and his shaggy hair fell over one eye. "My mom needs some help. We're uh, a little short-staffed right now."

"You own this place?"

"Yup. Todd Hart. H-a-r-t of Have-a-Hart Animal Shelter." He knelt down by the crate, and Morgan glimpsed a pack of cigarettes in his back pocket. "We're really full, but I'll find room for your kittens somewhere."

Morgan frowned. She didn't want her kittens crowded in with other bigger cats that might hurt them. "Can I see where you'll keep them?"

"Sure." He straightened, glanced at Morgan's other ear, stared at the floor, then looked at her chin. "You're Morgan Cross, aren't you?"

Morgan raised one eyebrow. "Do I know you?"

"No, but I go to Edgewood High. I'm in Maya's class, and I know your parents own the Gnosh."

"Do you hang out there?" she asked, racking her brain for some memory of him. He was polite but too geeky to be a friend of Maya's.

"No, too busy. I help Mom here. Since my dad died, we run

the family business ourselves." His voice trailed off. Then he lifted the crate. "Follow me."

Morgan opened the door for Todd, and the noise crescendoed. Barking mostly, but some squealing and growling and sounds of chewing. Morgan wrinkled her nose at the acrid smell. Cages needed cleaning somewhere.

As she followed Todd down the aisle between cages and pens, her heart sank. When he'd said they were full, he wasn't kidding. Overcrowded was more like it. Pens made from chain-link fence held three or four dogs each, pet carriers made for one cat held three or four, and glass aquariums held dozens of hamsters. Other animals ranged from rabbits to parakeets.

"Don't people adopt pets anymore?" Morgan finally asked, her alarm mounting. How could she leave her precious kittens here?

"They do, but it's been slow. This is a private shelter, and we have to make a profit too." Todd shrugged. "People can get free kittens and puppies from ads in the paper, so sometimes they don't want to pay the adoption fees or the cost to have their pet spayed or neutered."

Morgan made a snap decision. "You know, Todd, I've changed my mind. I'll keep the kittens."

"You sure?"

Morgan nodded. She'd never been more sure of anything in her life. She took the crate from him, thanked him for his time, and left. Outside at the car, Amber asked, "Won't they take them?"

"They would, but it's so overcrowded in there! Seems nobody's paying for kittens anymore."

"But you can't keep them," Amber said. "Your dad made a real point about that with me."

"Well, he didn't know the conditions here." Morgan slid the box into the backseat. "I'll figure out something else. I can find homes for them myself." She climbed into the front seat. "Please don't tell my dad yet."

"Oh, Morgan, I don't know. I'm not going to lie to him about this. He's my boss."

"You won't be lying. You can say I took care of the problem because I *will*. Please? I just can't leave them here. I could hardly stand to see the other animals in there, all crowded together in little stinky cages."

"Well, I don't like this, but I understand how you feel." Amber drove in silence for several blocks. "Okay, I won't say anything for now. But you have to figure something out soon."

"I promise! I'll get on it today." Back at home, Morgan jumped out of the car and retrieved her crate. "I'll keep them in the barn for now, till I find them homes. Thanks, Amber."

"You're welcome."

Morgan headed straight for the barn. It took her half an hour to fashion a sturdy pen of chicken wire for the kittens. After placing them inside, she got them two cans of tuna. She broke the tuna chunks into tiny bits and watched the animals eat till their tummies were stretched taut.

"You little pigs," Morgan said, grinning. "Be good till I get back."

At the house she grabbed a pack of peanut butter crackers from the kitchen, stuck it in her pocket, then hopped on her bike. Fifteen minutes later she rolled into Alex's driveway. She could see Alex's grandfather hoeing his vegetable garden out back. She knocked on the kitchen door.

"Come in!" Alex's grandma was at the counter kneading bread dough. "Hi, Morgan! How are you?"

"I'm good. Alex up?"

"Awake anyway. I heard music earlier. Go on up."

"Thanks." Upstairs, Alex was still in bed, playing with her own cat, Maverick. "Hey! What's up?" she said, leaning up on one elbow.

Morgan flopped on the foot of the bed and proceeded to tell her best friend about Zorro, her parents' orders, the overcrowded shelter, and Amber's promise not to squeal on her before she found homes for the kittens. "I need your help," she finished.

"With what?" Alex's words were nearly drowned out by a motorcycle zooming by.

Morgan glanced out the open window to the neighbor's house below. "Finding homes for the kittens, for one thing." She turned from the window. "If you'd seen that animal shelter, you'd be freaking out too. You know Todd Hart from school? He's in Maya's class. He and his mom run the shelter. I don't know if they can't afford to hire enough help or what, but they need more."

Alex yawned. "So?"

"So, how about if we volunteer there?"

"Are you crazy?"

"We could play with the animals and feed them and walk the dogs, fun stuff like that."

"Oh sure, and shovel out doggy-do and clean filthy hamster cages! And for no money! Ha!"

"Please? Just come with me once and see if you like it?"

Alex fell back on her pillows. "I'll hate it." She brushed her long frizzy hair back from her face. "On the other hand, what does this Todd look like?"

Morgan thought fast. Did she have to tell Alex that he was short, had shaggy hair, and smoked? "Well, he was very friendly," she said slowly, "and had lots of blond hair and a dark tan."

"Well, maybe I could volunteer there *once* and see—"

Just then barking erupted below Alex's window, followed by the crash of a garbage can being tipped over. "Not again!" Alex leaped from her bed and leaned out the window. "Get away from there! Go home!"

"What's going on?"

"Some dog keeps knocking over our trash cans and making a mess. Guess who gets to clean it up?"

"Alex!" her grandmother called up the stairs. "Oh, Alex!"

"See?" Alex pulled on cutoffs under her pajama shirt. "If I could catch him, I'd skin him."

"Alex!" Morgan cried. "He's just hungry!"

"Easy for you to say," Alex muttered, heading downstairs. "You don't have to clean up after him."

Outside, Alex grumbled as she stood the trash can upright, then refilled it with crumpled papers, greasy chicken bones, and potato peelings. "Man, what a mess."

Just then Alex's grandfather came around the corner of the house. "That will be the *last* time that dog gets in our trash."

"How do you know that?" Morgan asked.

"I just called Animal Control."

"The dogcatcher?" Morgan gasped. "He's just hungry!"

"Then let the dogcatcher feed him till someone claims him. He could have rabies or no telling what. Dangerous!" He stomped across the backyard toward his garden, watering can in hand.

Morgan was horrified. How could he be so cruel?

Alex jammed the metal lid down on the can and sniffed her hands. "El stinko." She wiped them on the seat of her shorts. "Want to sit on the porch?"

"No, I want to find that dog!" Morgan ran to the front yard and spotted a red collie as it dashed around the side of the neighbor's house, a meat wrapper in its mouth. At the same time, a white van with a picture of a dog on the side drove around the corner. "Oh, no!"

"Here, pooch! Come here!" Morgan called, glancing over her shoulder as the truck fast approached. "Come on!"

The collie eyed her suspiciously, the paper hanging from its jaws. Then Morgan remembered her peanut butter crackers. She quickly unwrapped them and held one out. The dog just watched. She took a big bite, then held the rest of it out to the dog. The collie trotted over to her just as the dogcatcher's van pulled into Alex's driveway.

A short, stocky man wearing thick black gloves climbed out of the van. "This the dog?" He came toward Morgan swinging a chain with a brown collar attached.

"That's the one," Alex called from the porch. "It gets in our garbage practically every day."

"You the one who called?"

"My grandpa did."

The dog ignored them all as it wolfed down the peanut butter cracker. Morgan slipped her arm around the collie's neck. It was filthy and needed brushing in the worst way, but underneath the tangled coat, she could see it was a beauty. The man reached for the dog, which snapped at his hand and growled. With one swift motion, the dogcatcher grabbed the dog's muzzle, squeezed it closed, then slipped on the collar. He dragged the dog toward the van and opened the double doors in the back.

"Wait!" Morgan said, running after him. "You can't take him!"

The dogcatcher turned around. "Why not?"

"Because—because he's my dog!"

chapter.4

The dogcatcher scratched his head. "Come again?"

Please forgive me, Morgan prayed. "Um, because it's not a stray. It's my dog."

"*Your* dog?" The man's voice was skeptical. "What's its name?"

Morgan swallowed hard. "Um, Jack."

"Oh really? Funny name for a female."

Morgan felt herself blush but walked toward the van. "Yes, well, it's short for, um, Jackie. You see, my friend's grandpa didn't know it was my dog when he called you." She knelt down beside the dog. "You can tell she's my dog. She knows me." Morgan hugged the dog's neck, and the collie licked her face.

"Doesn't appear you take very good care of her."

"Well, um, I've been gone, and she got loose. I was taking her home now. She won't bother these people ever again."

The man rocked back on his heels, glancing from Morgan to Alex to the dog. "Seems peculiar." Then he handed her the leash. "Keep your dog on a leash from now on. There are leash laws."

"Oh, I will, sir. Thank you, sir."

Alex joined Morgan by the driveway as the van drove away. "That was real bright. Just what are you going to do with this dog?"

"I'll find her a good home." Morgan buried her face in the collie's matted fur while it licked her hands, her knees, and her neck. "She can stay in the barn too."

"With the kittens? How smart is that?"

"There's room. I'll keep her in a horse stall. The kittens are in this pen thing I made from chicken wire." She stood and wrapped the leash twice around her hand. "Want to come help me?"

"I can't. I'm baby-sitting for the Teals today." Alex pushed back her bushy hair. "Your dad's going to catch you. You know that, don't you?"

"Not if I'm careful. He's working extra hours while Mom's gone. He never goes out to the barn anyway. I'll find homes for them before he notices a thing." Morgan pushed down the guilty thoughts that rose in her mind. She hated deceiving her dad. They'd always been close, and she wished she could ask for his help. If only he weren't so busy at the Gnosh Pit. She could really use his advice, but he had more important things to worry about than her strays. "I'll find homes for them," she repeated firmly.

Alex squatted down beside the collie. "Well, underneath the dirty fur, she *is* kind of pretty."

"You'd love the animals at the shelter too," Morgan coaxed. "Rabbits. Hamsters. Kittens. You should come with me."

Alex sighed and rolled her eyes. "When?"

"Tomorrow morning?"

"I'm not getting up early."

"Okay. Ten?"

"That's early."

"Eleven? I'll be here then."

Alex sighed again. "Okay. But I'm only going *once*, understand?"

Morgan nodded, but she knew that after Alex played with the animals there, she'd fall in love with them, too, and keep coming back. "See you in the morning."

When Morgan arrived home, she checked their neighbors on both sides, but everyone's shades were drawn against the sun. No kids were playing outside either. She hurried around back with the dog and headed for the barn. Inside, the kittens were awake and meowing. The collie growled deep in her throat.

"None of that. You're going to be great friends." Morgan kept a firm grip on the dog's collar and led her into the biggest horse stall. Thankfully, its walls were six feet high, too high for the dog to jump over, although she could see out through the gaps in the boards. "I'll bring you some food right away."

She bent down, unbuckled the collar, pushed the collie inside, and latched the door. Morgan would give her some sliced bologna, then bike to the store for some dog food and kitten food. Maybe a brush for the dog too. She still had last month's allowance. That should cover it.

She ran to the house for some sliced meat and a bowl of water, plus tuna for the kittens, but when she came back outside she heard a racket coming from the barn. She raced across the yard, slopping the water, and entered the barn.

"Stop that!" she called, slipping inside the horse stall. The collie immediately quieted down. "I brought you something." She set down the bowl of water, and the collie began lapping. Morgan took half a pound of bologna from the bag and placed it beside the water dish.

Then she popped the tops on three snack-size cans of tuna and fed the bits to the kittens. Four of them loved it. Zorro nibbled at one piece but couldn't seem to swallow it. Morgan frowned. She'd better get some kitten food soon.

She'd bike to the store right now, she decided. But when she got up to leave, the collie pressed her nose between two boards, crying and yelping. The lonely sound tore at Morgan's heart. The collie obviously wanted attention.

"Want to go for a walk?" Morgan said. Maybe she just needed some exercise, then she could sleep for a while. Morgan grabbed the dog's collar and leash from where she'd hung them on a nail and slipped into the horse stall. She nearly stepped in the water dish. Floating on top were bubbles of dog saliva and loose collie hair. *Ugh.*

The collie immediately jumped up, knocking Morgan sideways. "Down!" Morgan grabbed at the small red collie. "Down, girl!"

The dog's fluffy tail wagged crazily as she pushed her cold nose into Morgan's hand. Bracing herself to maintain her balance, Morgan wrapped her arm around the dog's neck and slipped on the brown collar. Sweat trickled down the sides of Morgan's face as she struggled to buckle it.

The collie jumped up and down, giving friendly barks and yelps. Whenever she came near Morgan's face, she delivered a sloppy lick.

"You're really lonely, aren't you, girl?" Pushing her hair back off her sweaty face, Morgan snapped on the red nylon leash. "Come on." Morgan wrapped the leash around her hand and stepped into the blinding June sunshine.

After the heavy rains all summer, the grass was spongy, and Morgan bounced as she walked. School had already been out for six weeks; yet every morning Morgan still felt a rush of pleasure, knowing she didn't have to go to school.

Crossing the long backyard, they passed the old playhouse, then the row of shrubs and trees that blocked the view of the house. Out front, the collie raced in circles around and around her feet, barking and yipping. "Stop that," Morgan said, pivoting in a circle three times to unwind the leash from her ankles. She glanced at the neighboring houses, ready with her story about walking a friend's dog should anyone ask. But both yards were empty.

Without warning, the collie leaped sideways toward the curb, then jerked abruptly on the leash as she changed direction and plunged forward. Morgan's neck snapped while her arm was nearly yanked from the socket.

Suddenly a gray squirrel raced across the sidewalk, causing the dog to bolt in the opposite direction. Morgan was whipped around, too, and she groaned and rubbed her sore shoulder muscle. At this rate, she'd have to borrow her dad's BenGay when she got home.

Gritting her teeth, Morgan tightened her sweaty grip on the leash. If only this dog would stop fighting her every step of the way and just *walk* like a normal, civilized animal! It took the excited collie four blocks to settle down, although every time she spotted a squirrel or bird or small child, she jumped and raced in circles. Morgan arrived home sore and drenched in sweat.

Wednesday morning, Morgan groaned when she rolled out of bed. Her right shoulder ached, and her arm muscles felt bruised as a result of walking the hyperactive collie. By eleven, she'd fed the kittens and dog with the food she'd bought the day before.

She biked to Alex's house when she finished. Alex was waiting outside, yawning between bites of a blueberry bagel.

"How do you talk me into stuff like this?" she grumbled, climbing on her bike.

"You'll thank me, you'll see," Morgan said. "You'll feel so good knowing you're helping these poor unwanted animals. I called the Harts yesterday and told them we were coming."

Alex only grunted and kept chewing.

Across town at the Have-a-Hart Animal Shelter, Morgan's shoulder ached just pulling open the front door. Inside, the office area was empty again, but the tinkling bell over the door eventually brought both Todd and a woman through the door at the rear.

"Hello! Can I help you?" the pleasant-looking woman asked.

"Mom, that's Morgan, the girl I was telling you about," Todd said. Suddenly he blushed. "I mean, you know, I mean the girl who called about volunteering."

Alex glanced sideways at Morgan, one eyebrow raised as if to say, *This is the tan blond guy you thought I'd want to meet? Ha!*

"And this is Alex," Morgan said. "We both wanted to volunteer. We'll do anything. Won't we, Alex?"

If looks could kill, Morgan would have keeled over. "Sure," Alex mumbled, "no problem."

"That's really wonderful!" the woman said. "I'm Lois Hart, the owner. This is an answer to my prayers. We're short-staffed, but we're also nearly at capacity. I'd be delighted to have you help out."

"Um, I can show them around." Todd smiled shyly at Morgan. Then he sneaked a quick peek at Alex, but her scowl made him retreat. "Morgan saw the animals yesterday, but her friend hasn't seen them."

"It's Alex," Alex said.

"Sorry, Alex." Todd stuck his hands in his back pockets.

Outside gravel crunched as a car pulled up. Mrs. Hart glanced out the window. "Todd, I need to finish the feedings. I'll show Alex around, and maybe she can help me finish up."

"Sure," Todd said.

Alex threw Morgan a *What am I doing here?* look, then followed Lois Hart through the rear door. At the same time, the front door opened, and a little boy stumbled in, carrying a box.

"Hey, Sammy!" Todd said. "What do you have for me today?" Hands on knees, he squatted by the young boy. "Morgan, this is Sammy Jenkins. He's one of our best customers."

"Hi," Morgan said, admiring his red hair and freckles.

"Hi." Sammy set his wooden box down on the floor. "Mom won't let me keep Snapper. I found him, but she won't let me keep him."

"Snapper?" Morgan eyed the box warily.

"My woodland turtle." The little boy grinned. "He doesn't really snap. I just call him that." He bent down and lifted the lid.

Morgan stared into the box. Resting on a flat rock in the corner, Snapper was about six inches long, with red feet and beady eyes. There was sand in the bottom of the box, plus a water dish and chunks of banana turning brown.

She glanced at Sammy. His face was a mixture of pride and sadness as he entrusted his cherished friend to them.

"Don't you worry," Todd said. "We'll take good care of Snapper."

"You'll like him," Sammy assured Morgan. "Remember to

change his water every day. He drinks funny. He sticks his snout in the water and sucks it up."

Morgan grinned as Sammy stuck his own nose in the air to demonstrate.

"And put Snapper in a sunny spot, okay?"

"We can put him by a window."

"Good. Do you have any corn on the cob? Snapper likes corn on the cob."

"I'll see what I can do." Todd stood and shook Sammy's hand. "We'll find him a good home."

"Promise?"

"Promise."

"Well, okay." Sammy turned and shook Morgan's hand too. "If Snapper gets scared, sing to him, okay? Then his head will come back out."

Morgan squeezed Sammy's grimy hand. "Sure. Anything special?"

"Nope. Just something fast and loud."

Morgan looked at the turtle, which had not moved since he was brought in. Yes, Snapper could use a peppy song. "Will do. Now don't worry about him."

"Okay." His expression downcast, Sammy backed toward the door. His eyes never left Snapper's box. Then in one quick movement, he was out the door.

Morgan smiled at Todd. "Will you really find a home for a turtle?"

"Sure, the same one I found for Sammy's snakes, salamanders, and tadpoles." He picked up the turtle's box. "Tonight I'll take him back down to the creek and turn him loose. Sammy won't know."

"I never thought an animal shelter would get salamanders and turtles."

"Oh, we get all kinds of animals here." He leaned on the counter. "Ever hear of a fainting goat? Or a Vietnamese potbellied pig?"

"You're kidding."

"I'm not. We've had both." He motioned behind him at the pet products on the shelves. "Even weirder is the stuff you can buy for pets."

Morgan read some of the labels aloud. "Low-calorie, low-cholesterol dog food? And carob-dipped dog biscuits?"

"That's nothing. There are special beds for dogs, too, even waterbeds. One's called a Wag Bag."

Morgan laughed. "On the Internet once I saw some doggy jogging suits advertised! There was even a doggy treadmill that mechanically walked the dog for the owner."

Todd slapped his hand on the counter. "I can top *that*. Some professor invented summer jackets for cows. The jackets protect the cows from the sun and biting insects."

"No way!"

He held up his right hand. "Scout's honor. I saw the article that showed the jacket. It covered the cow's head, back, and stomach. By wearing this jacket, the cow stays cooler. Then supposedly it will spend more time outside eating grass and making more milk."

Laughing, Morgan followed Todd and Snapper through the rear door into the main part of the shelter. She was immediately aware of the odor of pets confined too long, cages that needed cleaning, and pens that needed hosing down. As they walked back through the long building, which was really a series of smaller rooms joined in one long row, Morgan saw why Lois Hart was thrilled to have them volunteer. They might be doing the best they could, but the overcrowded animals were living in disgraceful conditions. It made Morgan sick at heart—and nearly sick to her stomach.

chapter.5

Morgan wished she could open a window to let in some fresh air, even if it was muggy, but she realized the air conditioning must be on, at least at a low level. She decided not to breathe too deeply. "What can I do to help?" she asked while Todd put the turtle by a window. "Exercise dogs? Clean cages?"

"Well, it's a smelly job, but the hamster and mice cages need cleaning, and the cat litter boxes too."

"Just point the way."

The first cage had an ID tag clipped to the door that said "Rex: angora rabbit." She poked her finger into the cage and wiggled it. "Hi, Rex." She reached inside to stroke the long-haired white rabbit with red eyes. She filled his water bottle from the bucket by the door, then pulled on gloves and scooped

42

up the scattered rabbit pellets, lettuce, and vegetable peelings to refill the feeding dish.

Closing the cage, she removed the newspaper from underneath Rex's hutch while she tried not to breathe, wadded it up, and replaced it with clean newspaper. She promised herself to brush his long "wool" the minute she finished with the other cages.

Morgan paused, then moved past the next cage, where a hamster slept inside his exercise wheel. The cage's ID tag said "Cinnamon." She'd save him for last, since Todd had warned that the hamster slept like he was in a coma and woke up real grouchy.

The next small cage was actually an aquarium holding a dozen or more variegated mice. Two were named Salt and Pepper, according to the tag. The skittery animals scurried back and forth. Morgan shuddered. Why in heaven's name would people choose rodents for pets?

Morgan was quick, but the mice were quicker, slipping easily through her fingers when she grabbed for them. It took six tries to capture the one she guessed was Pepper, and several more to catch Salt. She finally removed them all to a small dry bucket, then emptied and refilled their aquarium with fresh bedding. A noise behind her made Morgan turn around.

"Hi! How's it going?" Todd wheeled a cart that held bags of dog food.

"Great! I just wish I could adopt them all myself." She paused. "Well, maybe not the mice. Say, did you name all these animals yourself?"

"Hardly. See the name tags on each cage?" Todd pointed. "People bringing in animals fill them out. Sometimes they give their pets such stupid names."

Todd grinned then moved down the hall. Morgan added clean chlorophyll-treated shavings from a bag Todd showed her, then gave Salt, Pepper, and friends more cotton batting for nest material. She filled their dish with special food labeled "lab chow." Then she reached into a plastic bag for green twigs for the mice to gnaw on, so they wouldn't chew on their wire cage. Morgan noticed that they gnawed all the time. Todd had explained that their teeth grew constantly, and chewing kept them the right length.

Finished with the mice, Morgan backtracked to Cinnamon's cage.

"Time to rise and shine, fur ball." She lifted the sleepy hamster from his exercise wheel. He screeched and took a flying leap. Morgan caught him before he hit the floor, but his claws scratched as they slid down her arm. "Ow!" she cried, placing him in an empty box. He squawked and scolded as Morgan filled his water bottle and scooped the damp, dirty newspaper from the bottom of the cage. She nearly gagged. How long had it been since the cage was last cleaned? *Too* long, she knew.

Rubbing the red welts on her arm, Morgan read the tag on the last cage in the row. "Hello, Snowball." Inside, several small toys and wooden spools hung from strings for the cat to bat about. Morgan wished she had time to play with the kitten before changing his litter box. Even better, she wished Snowball could join her own strays in their roomy barn.

Twenty minutes later she'd finished cleaning the cages. She checked in the lobby, but didn't find anyone behind the counter. Morgan headed back through the center of the building to the rear, looking for Alex. As she wandered down the aisle between pens and dog runs, Morgan was struck again at how forlorn— and dirty—the animals looked. It was obvious that Todd and his mom just couldn't keep up. Morgan made up her mind. She'd volunteer to help at least three mornings a week for the rest of the summer. Hopefully she could persuade Alex to join her.

But when she found Alex a moment later, she knew her chances were zilch. Alex was in the last building, sweat dampening the back of her shirt. Mud smeared the front of her shirt and shorts.

"What happened to you?" Morgan asked.

Alex stood and arched her back as if it hurt. "That Lois," she hissed, "made me clean dog runs."

"Looks more like you've been mud-wrestling."

"I had to hose out the kennels, and the water ran to their pen outside. The dogs *loved* all that nice mud." She glared at Morgan. "I suppose you've been petting bunnies with Toddy for an hour?"

"I've been working too," Morgan said, although she'd obviously had more fun. "Let me find Todd and tell him we're leaving."

"And *never* coming back!" Alex snapped.

Morgan didn't answer but continued down the hallway. Near the back she found a door marked Storeroom that was slightly ajar. She pushed it open a few inches, and wrinkled her nose at the smell of cigarette smoke. "Todd?"

"Just a minute."

She stepped in, glancing at shelves that held a few bags of cat food and pet supplies. Morgan was surprised. Surely it took a bigger inventory of supplies to care for this many animals. Near the open window, Todd hurriedly crushed a cigarette on the cement floor. Looking sheepish, he fanned the smoke out the window. "I'm trying to quit. Don't mention this to my mom, okay?"

"I won't." She stood awkwardly. Somewhere a phone rang three times, then quit. "I just came to tell you that Alex and I are going home now. I finished those cages."

"Great!" He followed her out of the storage room and closed the door. Ducking his head and avoiding her eyes, he said, "Thanks for the help."

"You're welcome. I really love animals."

By the time they reached the lobby, Alex was already slouched on the floor near the door, her mud-smeared legs stretched out ahead of her. Lois Hart stood at the counter, frowning as she talked on the phone. She turned then and saw Morgan.

"Wait a moment, please," she said into the phone, then covered the mouthpiece with her hand. "Thanks so much for helping, girls! I appreciate it!"

"You're welcome," Morgan said.

"Yeah," Alex grunted.

Outside, they grabbed their bikes from the rack in the parking area. There were only two cars there. Morgan figured both belonged to the Harts. The van had a big red heart painted on the side, but the black car next to it had an orange-and-yellow fireball streaking down the side. *Lovely.*

Morgan decided to ignore Alex's scowl. She chattered on and on about Rex the angora rabbit, Cinnamon the hamster, the mice, and even Todd's story about the cow coats. "I just wish there was more I could do," Morgan said, running out of breath. "I want to adopt them all."

"You'd better hurry up then." Alex's hair flew back over her shoulders. "Their days are numbered. Like *doomed.*"

"What're you talking about?"

"Mrs. Hart was on the phone when I came into the room, but it was a long time before she noticed me. I overheard her say the shelter's closing."

"Closing! Why?"

"No money to run it. People aren't paying their prices to adopt pets. Mrs. Hart also said something about having to pay a big hospital bill. Have-a-Hart is bankrupt, or nearly."

"Bankrupt!" They stopped at a red light, then pedaled across the intersection. Morgan was so deep in thought that she nearly rear-ended Alex. So that's why the storeroom shelves were nearly empty. "Did you hear when they were closing?"

"On Monday."

"Less than a week!"

"Yup. She was arranging for the animals to be transported to the county pound in Blairsburg." At the next intersection, they went their separate ways. Alex yelled back over her shoulder, "And you know what happens at the pound. Put to sleep. *Permanently.*" She turned and pedaled off down the street toward her home.

Morgan's heart was in her throat. The county pound? Snowball, Rex, Cinnamon—all put to sleep? No! She couldn't allow that! There had to be something she could do. There just had to be. For the next four blocks she racked her brain for a workable idea to save the shelter animals. What could she do? *What?* She had less than a week before they were transferred, but somehow, Morgan would find a way to rescue them.

It was truly a matter of life and death.

chapter.6

Morgan was still deep in thought when she got home. She was surprised to find Amber's mom's car parked in her driveway. What was Amber doing there? Morgan frowned. Had her dad tried to call her then sent Amber to check on her when she didn't answer the phone?

Morgan knew the house was locked, so Amber must be in back. Morgan parked her bike and headed around the house. She stopped short. No one was on the patio either, but from the barking coming from the barn, she guessed where Amber was. Morgan trotted across the yard toward the barn. Inside, she found Amber just as she expected, but Bren was with her too.

"Get down!" Bren snapped. "I mean it!" The young collie slurped her hand, her bare leg, then her arm. "Get that dog away from me! Look at my shorts! Dog hair! And dog slime on my legs."

"Sorry." Amber pulled the dog closer, then glanced up. "Morgan! Where were you?"

"Volunteering at the shelter. What're you doing?"

"I just came by to see if you'd found homes for the kittens, and there was such a racket coming from out here! Where'd you get the dog?"

Morgan glanced at Bren, worried that yet another person knew her secret. "You guys have to promise not to tell Dad."

"I haven't. Not yet anyway." Amber dropped down cross-legged on the barn floor, and the collie draped herself across Amber's lap.

"What's to tell?" Bren asked. "Where'd the mutt wander in from?"

"It's a stray I rescued from the dogcatcher. I'll find a home for her while I find homes for the kittens." Morgan collapsed on an overturned metal bucket. "I don't know how though. Even the shelter can't find enough good homes. Alex heard they're closing. In less than a week they're sending all their pets to the county pound! I wish I could find homes for them all!"

Amber coaxed the collie back into the horse stall, but the animal barked so loud that Bren covered her ears. "This is how loud it sounded before."

Morgan rubbed her throbbing forehead. "Maybe she's just lonely by herself."

"'Music soothes the savage beast,'" Bren quoted.

"What?" Morgan asked.

"Music. Bring your radio out here and play some tunes." She turned slowly. "There's an outlet by the light switch to plug it in."

Amber pulled her hair back into a ponytail. "It's worth a try. Otherwise you'll never keep your dad from finding her before you adopt her out."

Morgan sighed. "I'll see what 'soothing dog music' I can find. Be right back." At the house she let herself in the back door. Inside, the answering machine beeped. She hit the *Play* button.

"Hi! This is Cheryl next door. Say, do you have a dog now? Somebody's dog barked all morning and sounded kind of frantic. Thought you might want to know, if it's yours." *Beee-eeep.*

Oh man, Morgan thought, hitting *Erase.* Complaining neighbors were the last thing she needed. She took the carpeted stairs two at a time up to her room to find some music for the barn. She grabbed her portable stereo, then took five CDs from her mom's collection in the den—what her dad called "elevator music." It ought to put anything to sleep.

Back in the barn, she plugged in the stereo and set it to play the CDs randomly. Soon the barn was filled with soft, boring music. No sound at all came from the dog. Morgan sank to the floor of the barn.

"You look beat," Amber said. "Can I help?"

"You want to adopt any of these guys?"

"Wish I could. Are you sure you can't ask your dad for help? I know he'd want you to."

Morgan chewed on her upper lip. "He's got enough to handle with Mom and Maya gone. I don't want to bother him."

"Well, I have to say that I don't feel right about this. I don't like deceiving your dad. He thinks I took those cats to the animal shelter."

"Well, you did!" Morgan said. "You just didn't leave them there. Anyway, I can't afford to keep them long. It took all my allowance to buy dog and cat food."

"This is all just too, too fascinating," Bren said, brushing dog hair from her shirt, "but that canine ruined my outfit. I need to go home and change."

"Now?" Amber asked.

"Yes, now. I can hardly go to the mall smelling like dog spit."

Amber sighed. "I'll drop you. I have to get down to the Gnosh anyway. Promised I'd help Benny do salads before the supper shift."

Morgan followed them out of the barn. "Bye. And thanks for keeping my secret."

That night her dad dragged in late, barely spoke, and headed straight for the shower. In Maya's room Morgan logged on for the TodaysGirls chat. Since Maya had taken the laptop, Morgan was free to use the computer in her sister's room. While it officially belonged to Maya, Morgan, and their older brother, Maya hogged it 102 percent of the time.

It took just a moment to find and click the bookmark, then

wait while *Welcome to TodaysGirls.com* appeared on her magenta screen. Amber's Thought for the Day popped open automatically. Morgan knew the minute she read it exactly who Amber was talking to.

Look at the birds in the air. They don't plant or harvest or store food in barns. But your heavenly Father feeds the birds. Matthew 6:26

Nothing is too small for our heavenly Father to care about and help you with! He cares for the animals--and he cares for you!

Morgan figured that was true, but she assumed God expected her to do her share. God had the whole world to take care of, after all. She'd find homes for the strays herself.

Morgan clicked the chat room icon and watched the screen flicker, then load. Everyone was there except Maya. Excellent!

jellybean: hey, GFs! when Maya gets here, don't talk
　about my strays. I can't have her tell dad and mom B4
　I find homes 4 them
TX2step: what's UR plan?
faithful1: could U post ads on the internet? it's free. U
　had good luck using pet sites B4 for other stuff
jellybean: maybe. I don't know?????????????

Morgan sat back then and watched her friends' words appear and scroll up the screen. Amber's suggestion to post ads online was a good idea. Morgan snapped her fingers. Half a good idea anyway!

chicChick: teach them some manners first. that dog ruined my shorts

TX2step: YOUR shorts? u should C what I looked like after Morgan forced me 2 work @ that shelter today. cleaned 8 dog kennels. P U!!

chicChick: teach you 2 go there. Disease city! I had a hamster once, no a gerbil, and I got scaly stuff on my hands that flaked off like leprosy or something. like I tried hand lotion and baby oil, but it peeled in layers!

rembrandt: Morgan, the Gnosh was swamped 2nite. I saved some steak bones and gravy

jellybean: thanks!!!!!

chicChick: is this like a pet chat room now? Like hello! did anybody see Alecia's new 2 piece today? what is that woman thinking? it was so stretched out of shape! But that new lifeguard! Whoa! hold me back!

Morgan's mind wandered as she considered Amber's suggestion. What if she did more than post Internet ads? Instead of posting ads on other people's Web sites, why couldn't she have a Web page of her *own*? An online adopt-a-pet Web site? She bet

Amber would be willing to help set it up. After all, Amber had done the TodaysGirls.com Web site, and it hadn't looked that hard.

Morgan was just about to type her question to Amber when *nycbutterfly enters the room* appeared on her screen. *Maya!*

nycbutterfly: hello lucky people. i'm here

jellybean: whazzup? U surviving?

nycbutterfly: barely. this place is a haunted house. no wonder Rose won't stay here

chicChick: Rose?

nycbutterfly: Great Aunt Rose. she owns it now but is selling. we're sorting through boxes and old clothes and pictures.

chicChick: yuck and double yuck

nycbutterfly: it's not that bad really. U should C some of the clothes. silk floor-length dresses. lace shawls. cool hats. Rose says I can have what I want.

jellybean: when R U coming home?

nycbutterfly: missing me, li'l sis?

jellybean: I cry myself 2 sleep every nite

Actually she wanted to know how much time she had to find homes for the strays. If Maya and Mom stayed in Johnston long enough, and if Amber helped her set up an adoption Web site, she could bring home the animals from the shelter too. She'd find them homes to keep them from getting shipped to the pound. If only Maya and Mom would stay put!

> **nycbutterfly:** mom says we'll come home in a week or 10 days
>
> **chicChick:** U might as well B in jail!!!!!!
>
> **nycbutterfly:** it's not so bad really. we eat out every night. Rose tells the funniest stories. she's ancient-- 60 something--and wears pink jogging suits!

The words on the screen blurred together as Morgan's mind whirled a hundred miles a minute. She had over a week, maybe ten days, to put an adoption Web site to work. She knew Edgewood had its own Web site—the Gnosh had an advertisement on it. Maybe Amber could link Morgan's pet adoption site to it somehow. She'd e-mail her privately right after the chat.

Since Morgan wouldn't charge for adopting out the animals, they ought to find homes quickly. First thing tomorrow she'd tell Lois Hart that she wanted the shelter pets. She'd have to save them all! She could hardly save a few and let the others be shipped off to an uncertain fate.

As soon as the chat was over, Morgan e-mailed Amber, outlining her idea for a Web site to advertise pets to adopt. She tried to be as persuasive as possible.

Call me first thing in the morning. Please!

Finished, she clicked *Send*.

Just then her dad poked his head into Maya's room. "Still chatting?"

"Just finished." Morgan grinned at her dad's dripping hair and Jacob's cast-off shorts and T-shirt. Her brother's clothes looked weird on her dad.

He padded in and stood behind her, hands on her shoulders. "How you doing? Missing those kittens?" he asked, stifling a yawn.

Guilt stabbed her, and Morgan evaded the question. "Alex and I volunteered at the animal shelter today. I loved it."

He yawned again, louder. "Will you go back?"

"Yup, but not Alex. She hated it." Thinking of the bankrupt shelter, Morgan took a deep breath. Maybe Amber was right. Maybe she ought to tell her dad about the problem. She opened her mouth to speak, but her dad's words cut her off.

"I'm bushed," he said, rubbing his hand through his wet hair.

"Hey, you're sprinkling me!" Morgan said, laughing.

"Sorry, honey." He stepped back. "I just came in to say good night actually. And to tell you I'm going in real early tomorrow to do paperwork. I can get twice as much accomplished if I work before the restaurant actually opens."

Morgan could see how exhausted he was, and she forced a smile. "Okay. Good night."

After he left, Morgan turned back to the computer. What should a pet adoption site look like? Maybe she could find a model online and create something similar. At the Google search engine, she typed in "pet adoptions," "animal shelters," and "animal rescues." In just minutes she had a dozen sites to check out.

Rummaging in Maya's desk, she found a pen and scratch pad and started making notes. The Pet Adoption Project was a free service "dedicated to helping match pets in animal shelters with the people who want to adopt." Photos of dogs and cats, along with their names, filled several pages. Another site called Safe Sanctuary was a network of foster homes where animals could recover from abuse, both physical and emotional. It claimed to be a "place where the animals' bodies and spirits are made whole again, where trust is reawakened through compassionate care." Morgan *loved* the sound of that. That's exactly what she wanted her strays to feel like.

For the next hour she toured sites like Petsville, a group of organizations dedicated to helping animals; the Exotic Bird Rescue site, a group dedicated to the rescue and placement of unwanted, mistreated, and neglected exotic birds; and Caring Control, which sold special animal cages for catching sick animals and raccoon traps to "solve any wild pet problem."

It was after eleven when she closed the last site. Checking her e-mail, Morgan was excited to see a message from Amber.

Your plan sounds great! I can be over in the morning to set up your site, but I have to waitress at 11. Decide on a name for your site and write the ad you want. Be sure

you give your phone number and e-mail address in the ad so people can contact you. I've got the Web design software, the same we used for TodaysGirls. We can use the same free Web host. I have clip art too. See you at 8? Too early? Let me know. Amber

"Yes!" Morgan knew nothing about Web design software or Web hosting, but then, that's why she'd asked Amber. She clicked *Reply*.

8 is great! Dad's going in really early. THANK YOU SO MUCH!!!!! See you in the morning. Morg

She clicked *Send*, waited, then closed down the computer. Suddenly she was pooped.

Still, she needed to make some notes before she went to bed. Then Amber could get right to work in the morning designing the site. She'd mentioned clip art. Morgan hoped that meant animal pictures or cartoons. It would make her page more appealing since she had no way to put actual photos of the animals online.

Another hour passed as Morgan scribbled and crossed out and rewrote her ad. She'd tried several names but finally settled on the Pet Place. Her ad read: "Come to the Pet Place in Edgewood where barking and meows are signs of joy, where loneliness is replaced by love, where animals wait for a permanent home. The owners of the Pet Place really LOVE these animals, holding and playing with them daily. Pets live in a warm, dry barn with plenty of space. All pets are FREE and guaranteed child-friendly. Your perfect pet is waiting!"

At the end Morgan listed her first name, their teen line phone number, e-mail address, and the hours she would be "open by appointment." She only wanted customers coming when her dad was at work.

Although she was exhausted when she finally fell into bed, Morgan slept fitfully. Every time she closed her eyes and drifted off, she'd dream of the shelter animals, starving, skinny, and dirty. Morgan woke up the next morning more tired than when she'd collapsed the night before.

If only she could keep the nightmare from becoming a reality.

chapter.7

Thursday morning at eight, Amber arrived with the plastic bag of Gnosh leftovers. Morgan put them in the refrigerator before they headed upstairs. "I brought two CDs, software, and art," Amber explained. At the computer, she read Morgan's ad and grinned. "This is great. Warm and friendly, but professional."

"You think so?"

"Just leave it to me now. We'll do something simple with a template . . ." Pulling her blonde hair back in a ponytail, she leaned over Morgan's notes. "I should be able to publish this online before I go to work."

"*Really?*"

"Sure. With templates, you choose a form you like, then decide on colors, text, and graphics. Sort of a fill-in-the-blank test."

Her hopes high, Morgan watched Amber for the next two hours and chose colors and clip art. She was amazed at how fast it went together. The Web page background was a textured tan, the ad itself was in black, with a black paw print border. A brown puppy curled up next to a gray-striped cat beside large green letters announcing "The Pet Place."

"Here's your Web address," Amber said when she finished. "I'll bookmark it for you." Then, glancing at her watch, she pushed back from the computer. "Still fifteen minutes till I have to be at work!"

"Thanks so much!" Morgan said. "This looks great. You should hire out doing Web sites for people."

"You're sweet." Amber tightened her ponytail. "I don't do anything fancy though. Anybody can do it with the software."

"*I* couldn't! I just know this will help me find good homes."

"I hope so. Just be patient. You won't show up on the search engines overnight."

"What's that mean?"

"Well it takes weeks—even months sometimes—for your site to show up in a search."

"I don't have that much time!" Morgan collapsed onto Maya's bed. "How will people find my pet site then?"

Amber leaned her chin on her fist and frowned. "Well, it won't really matter if your site shows up on search engines around the world. You just want people fairly close to Edgewood to know about it, people willing to drive here to get animals."

"How do I do that?" Morgan chewed her upper lip. This was getting more complicated by the minute.

Suddenly Amber snapped her fingers. "Wait one sec. I need something from my car." In less than a minute she'd gone to her car and was back. She unfolded and spread a map of Indiana on the floor. "Now," she said, grabbing a pencil, "how far will people be willing to drive to adopt a pet, do you suppose?"

"An hour?" Morgan asked. "More? I don't know."

Amber drew a rough circle with Edgewood at the center and the circumference about fifty miles out. She handed Morgan the pencil. "Write down these names." Amber read the names of towns, small and large, within the circle. "Now, look them up on the Internet. Just put the *www* in front of each town's name, and a *.com* after it, like www.Edgewood.com, and see what you get."

"But why?"

"If you turn up a Web site for any of these towns, then find the link for its Chamber of Commerce. That group publicizes stuff. Write each chamber and tell them about your adoption site here in Edgewood, give them your Web address, and ask them to post your link on their Web site. Some of them will do it to beef up their sites. Then the people in surrounding towns will hear about your site faster."

"I never would have thought of that. Thanks!"

"No problem. This was fun." Amber grabbed her bag. "Gotta run. Keep me posted."

After she left, Morgan e-mailed Jamie.

Thanx for the steak bones and stuff. Amber brought them over this a.m. Check out the new site Amber built for me at www.ThePetPlace.com. Can you keep saving food scraps? Without dad getting suspicious, I mean? Thanx! Morgan

After pressing *Send*, Morgan pulled on her tennis shoes, grabbed the bag of leftovers from the fridge, and headed to the barn. Thank goodness her dad was so busy at work right now. He left early and was home after dark, when even the dog and kittens were asleep.

The collie wolfed down some meat scraps. Morgan filled a bowl with pet chow for the kittens. As she watched them eat, Morgan gazed around the dim barn. With the sky overcast, the filtered sunlight made it hard to see into the shadows. The single weak light bulb overhead was no help. Nearly three-fourths of the barn was still empty. She could build pens and cages for another dozen animals maybe. With the Pet Place adoption site up, she could now move into Phase Two of her plan.

After refilling both dishes with fresh water, she ran back to the house, made some toast and buttered it, then hopped on her bike. As she ate on the way to the Have-a-Hart Animal Shelter, an idea formed in her mind.

"Hi, Todd, is your mom around?" Morgan asked when she burst through the front door.

Before he could speak, Lois Hart stood up from behind the

counter. "Hi, Morgan. What can I do for you?" Then she disappeared again.

Morgan leaned over the counter to talk to the woman who squatted beside an open filing cabinet. "I wanted to volunteer again for a couple hours."

"That's wonderful! Todd can show you what needs doing."

Morgan cleared her throat. "Before that, I want to ask you something."

"Sure. What?"

"I want to adopt a lot of your pets. We have room at home—we've got an empty barn—and I love animals. I'd take really good care of them."

Todd moved to stand beside her, and Morgan wrinkled her nose at the faint cigarette smell. If his mom weren't standing right there, Morgan would lecture him on the hazards of smoking. Didn't he know he was asking for lung cancer?

"How many animals did you want?"

"Well, um, maybe a dozen. More, if they're small. All the small ones for sure. I could take them home with me today." Morgan smiled, sure that she could get Amber to help her transport them.

Lois Hart stood slowly, her eyes open wide. "That's wonderful, but it's going to be pretty expensive."

Morgan's jaw dropped. "Why? Aren't they free?"

"Well technically, yes." Mrs. Hart showed her a clipboard with a fee list on it. "But there's a processing fee, and money paid for getting the animals spayed or neutered, and for getting their shots. There are requirements to meet before we adopt out our pets to ensure their health."

"Oh." Morgan's allowance would never cover that. "How about if I work more volunteer hours in trade for the animals?"

Todd drummed his fingers on the counter. "What about it, Mom? They'd go to a good home this way."

Morgan held her breath. She didn't want to reveal to the Harts that she knew they were going out of business and shipping the animals to the pound soon.

Mrs. Hart finally nodded. "It's apparent that you love the animals, too, Morgan. I guess that would be okay."

Morgan let out the breath she'd been holding. "Oh thank you!"

Lois Hart handed Todd several sheets of paper. "Fill these out for Morgan with the names of the animals she wants to take home." She pointed to the bottom line. "Morgan, since you're under eighteen, I'll need a parent's signature there."

Morgan's heart fell. *A parent's signature?* She stared blindly at the forms. She couldn't ask her dad about this! He'd never agree. And yet, she couldn't just walk away and leave these poor animals to face an almost certain death at the county pound either. "No problem. I'll take the papers home with me today."

Morgan folded the papers and stuck them in her pocket, then followed Todd back to the small animal cages, half listening to him while she helped feed them. When they ran out of lab chow, he sent Morgan to the storeroom for another bag.

Down the hall beyond the dog runs, Morgan let herself into the storage room. Grabbing the bag of food, she was surprised to hear rain pattering against the small window. She looked outside, then got spattered by a gust of wind that blew rain against the screen. She pulled the window down, shaking her head. She bet Todd had left it open again after smoking in there. Why didn't he just go outside instead of hiding in the storeroom? A smoky smell clung to his clothes. Did he really think he was fooling his mom?

By the time Morgan was ready to leave an hour later, the rain had stopped and steam rose from the hot pavement as she pedaled home. Deep in thought about the shelter animals' fate, she glided through an intersection without looking, then nearly crashed when a car honked and swerved to miss her. Her heart thumping, she continued down the street. The air felt like a sauna, and Morgan was grateful to let herself into her air-conditioned house.

The message light on their teen phone was blinking, and Morgan pressed a button as she headed to the fridge for some juice.

"Hello. Is this the Pet Place?" a nasal voice asked. Morgan's hand froze on the refrigerator handle. She already had a customer! "This is Gloria Engles. Please call me back immediately." And she gave her phone number. Morgan scrambled for a pencil and the notepad by the phone, scribbling as the message finished.

Before she could call Ms. Engles back, the phone rang. Morgan grabbed the phone. "Hello? Cross residence."

"Rats. I was calling the Pet Place," a young-sounding boy said.

"Oh! This is the Pet Place too. Can I help you?"

"Yeah! At least, I hope so." His breathless voice had a faint accent. "I'm looking for a dog. What kinds do you have?"

"Well, right now I just have a small red collie, but I may have more soon. The collie is beautiful though, and very friendly."

"I love collies!"

"Do your parents know you want a dog?"

"Yeah! We've looked at different places, but I haven't found what I wanted. I'd love a collie though."

Great! A winner already! Morgan thought. "Well, you'll want to come visit her to make sure you like her." Her mind raced. This boy's family had to come before her dad got home from work.

"Should we bring a truck?" he asked.

"Not unless your parents won't let her in the car. She's not that big."

"We don't have a car."

"Oh, well, then a truck is fine. Can you come before four o'clock?"

"Probably. I'll buy tickets now. I know where to buy tickets online."

"Tickets for what?"

"To fly to your state."

Morgan frowned. Someone out of state had seen her site? "Where *are* you?" she asked.

"Mars." The young boy snorted.

Morgan rolled her eyes. "How old are you?"

"Ten. How old are you, turkey?"

"Hey!" She was cut off when he slammed the phone down in her ear. *Good grief.* Morgan was pouring her juice when the phone rang again. "Hello?" she said.

"Hello. Is this the Pet Place?"

"Yes, that's me. I mean, I'm Morgan, and that's my Web site."

"My name is Gloria Engles, and I live in Edgewood. I left a message for you a while ago?"

"Yes, I was about to call you back."

"A family emergency requires that I leave town for a few days. I have a pet, a special pet, that I need someone to watch. Your ad sounded different, like you really care for animals."

"Oh, yes, I really do." Morgan frowned. "But I don't baby-sit animals. I'm adopting them out."

Ms. Engles sighed. "I know, but I'm desperate. I have no nearby neighbors to leave him with. Couldn't you watch Glamour Boy for three—maybe four—days? I'd pay you."

"Glamour Boy?"

"My Peruvian guinea pig. He's quite distinctive and has won many first prizes and blue ribbons in competition. I assume your facility is air-conditioned?"

"Well, no, it's a barn. It's totally shaded though. Anyway, I don't know—"

"Shaded? Hmm. You'd have to promise, if it turns hot, that

you'll bring Glamour Boy inside where it's cool. Do you promise?"

Morgan rubbed the back of her neck. A good breeze usually blew through the open hayloft doors, but she could probably sneak the guinea pig into the basement if the temperature shot up. "I guess I could, but—"

"He's a well-behaved, obedient guinea pig. He has his own cage and food. You won't have a bit of trouble with him."

"Yes, but—"

Then Ms. Engles named a fee high enough to make Morgan blink. It would pay for a lot of food for her strays—and for the ones she hoped to bring home from the shelter. "When can you bring him out here?" Morgan asked, figuring quickly. Her dad had said he wouldn't be home till late that night. "Can you come this afternoon?"

"Actually I need to bring him out right away." Ms. Engles sniffled and blew her nose. "There's been an emergency. My parents, you know. Just last night. I'm leaving on a long drive immediately."

"I didn't realize—"

"Can I bring Glamour Boy out right now? I've already packed my bags. I'll leave him with you on my way out of town." She double-checked Morgan's address. "Thank you so much. You can't know how I appreciate this."

Twenty minutes later Morgan saw a long boat-like car glide into their driveway. She jogged across the backyard and rounded the corner of the house. A short, plump woman in her fifties crawled out from under the steering wheel, opened the back door, and removed a glittery royal-blue cage.

Morgan brushed dog hair off her shirt, walked to the car, and held out her hand. "I'm Morgan Cross." She nodded at the cage. "This must be Glamour Boy."

"Yes, it is." The plump lady sniffled and blinked her puffy, red eyes. "I can't thank you enough for taking care of him. He's my family, you know. He goes everywhere with me, so I'm sure he doesn't understand why I must leave him behind this time. But with the hospital and everything, you know . . ." Her wobbly voice trailed off, and her eyes filled with tears.

"I'll take extra good care of him. Don't worry about a thing," Morgan assured her, reaching for the cage.

She pried the handle from the woman's trembling hand, pulled aside the quilted cover, and nearly dropped the cage. Morgan couldn't believe her eyes.

Inside, sitting on a quilted pillow, was the hairiest animal she'd ever seen. Morgan squinted and peered closer. She couldn't even tell which end was which. Long silky hair completely covered its head, face, and plump, short-legged body.

"How in the world do you keep all this hair so neat?"

"I brush him every day, of course. Then, before competitions, I shampoo it. I put his hair in rollers, too, so it flips up nicely on the ends."

A guinea pig in rollers? Using all the will power Morgan could muster, she forced herself to keep a straight face. It wouldn't be right, with this lady all worried, to burst out laughing.

"How often do you feed him?"

"Just once a day, in the morning." Ms. Engles tried to smile, and her small mouth trembled. "If you don't feed him on time, he'll squeal at you. Or whistle."

"Whistle? For his food?"

"Yes, and like all Peruvian pigs, he honks too. Glamour Boy really likes his food."

I do too, Morgan thought, setting the carrier on the grass. *Maybe I should try whistling and honking for it.*

Before she could think of a suitable reply, a movement at the intersection caught her eye. Alex swung around the corner on her bike, headed for Morgan's house. She pulled up and stopped beside them a minute later.

"Hey, Alex." Morgan nodded at the older lady. "This is Ms. Engles. She's leaving her guinea pig for me to watch for a few days."

Alex bent over the cage, then snorted aloud. "That's a guinea pig? You're joking, right?" She squatted down to get a better look. "Which end is which? Looks more like a dust mop that lost its handle."

Ms. Engles gasped.

Morgan gave Alex a warning nudge with her toe. "This is a prize-winning guinea pig that's won *lots* of competitions. It's no ordinary pet."

"That's correct, young lady." Ms. Engles fixed Alex with a poisonous glare. "Judges across the country have given my Glamour Boy blue ribbons. He's most unusual."

"No kidding," Alex said. "I've never seen such a—"

"Thank you for coming," Morgan interrupted. "Glamour Boy will be fine. Just leave everything to me, and don't worry."

Ms. Engles cast a longing look at Glamour Boy, then turned and reached into her car for a shopping bag. "I should be back on Monday. His toys are in the bag, as well as plenty of his special pellets and some piggy treats."

"Piggy treats?" Morgan blinked.

"Supernutritious snacks for guinea pigs. They're shaped like little stars. *Ordinary* guinea pigs eat raw vegetable peelings and grass. They even chew on green twigs." She sniffed. "Not my Glamour Boy. He needs special care." She opened the bag wider. "With the weather warm, you probably won't need them, but I also brought along his hooded sweatshirt and an extra blanket, just in case the nights turn nippy."

Alex opened her mouth to say something, but Morgan sent her a pleading look. Alex's mouth snapped shut.

Finally, after Ms. Engles repeated her instructions three times and blew a kiss to Glamour Boy, she drove away. Alex watched her leave, then knelt and opened the guinea pig's cage door. First she lifted the long silky hair on one end of the animal, then the other.

"Hey, I found the head. Want me to mark it for you?"

"Alex, close the cage." Morgan dropped the shopping bag on the grass. "Did you stop for anything special?"

"Just to see how your morning at the shelter went and see if you wanted to go to the pool." She laid her mesh towel bag near her bike on the grass. "What gives? I thought you were getting rid of animals, not adopting more."

"I'm not adopting this thing. Amber helped me set up a Web site to adopt the strays out, and that lady saw my site and called to ask if I'd watch her guinea pig. She offered to pay me thirty dollars for just a few days!" She peered into the shopping bag. "Since it brought its own food, it won't cost me anything but a little time. I can really use the money to buy food for the strays."

"I guess. Want to go swimming?"

Morgan sighed. "I wish I could, but I promised Dad I'd come down to bus tables for the supper crowd. Want to come in and see the Web site Amber set up for me?"

Alex glanced overhead. "For a minute. Then I'm heading to the pool."

Morgan stashed Glamour Boy's carrier in a corner of the barn, away from the dog and kittens, then showed Alex her Web site. "If I had a digital camera, I could add photos of the pets I have to give away. I think that would help."

"Did you get any calls besides that guinea pig owner?"

"One. A boy who turned out to be from Mars."

"A bit of a hike to come for a pet."

"Let me check my e-mail though. Probably a lot of people

will use e-mail instead of the phone." Before she did that, Morgan whipped over to TodaysGirls.com to see if Jamie or Amber was in the chat room. It was empty, although Amber's Thought for the Day was another one obviously addressed to Morgan.

God takes care of ALL his creatures--and that means YOU too! "Look at the sea, so big and wide. Its creatures large and small cannot be counted. . . . All these things depend on you to give them their food at the right time." Psalm 104:25, 27

Morgan sighed. That verse only applied to wild animals, she was sure. The ones in her barn—and even at the shelter—depended on *her* to give them food and find them homes. God had enough wild animals to worry about. The least she could do was her share for the domesticated ones.

Morgan clicked her e-mail icon and watched four messages load. The first one was from Maya and copied to each TodaysGirl.

I am DESPERATE to talk to everyone! PLEASE meet in chat room today at 3!!!!!

What was that all about, Morgan wondered uneasily. The second message was from Jamie.

Sure I'll save more food at work. Benny leaves before clean-up, and your dad won't notice. Hey, the next time Coach comes in with his boys, want me to convince him to get his kids a dog? I bet I could! See ya LTR. Jamie.

Morgan frowned. "She'd better not say anything to Coach in front of my dad."

"Don't worry," Alex said. "She'd never tell where the stray came from."

The third e-mail was from someone she didn't know.

How many kittens do you have? Are they weaned? We only want Siamese cats. Please respond.

Morgan sighed. Siamese? She clicked *Reply*.

I have five kittens to give away, but none are Siamese. They ARE beautiful, well-behaved kittens though. Very unusual markings. One has a mask. Would you like to see them anyway? Morgan Cross, Owner of the Pet Place.

Alex kicked off her flip-flops and fell across Maya's bed. "Did you go back to the shelter today?"

Morgan whirled around. "Yes, I almost forgot." She shook her head slowly. "I asked Mrs. Hart's permission to bring some animals home. She said I could work extra hours to pay the adoption fees, but Dad needs to sign a release form, like a permission slip, because I'm under eighteen."

"Fat chance of that."

"No joke. I'm not giving up though. There has to be a way to rescue them before they get shipped off."

"Morgan, you can't save every animal in town. Face it."

"I know that! But I have to do everything I *can!*" She turned back and opened her fourth message. She read slowly. "Hey, listen to this one. 'Saw your local ad. Need someone to watch child's pet for a week while on vacation. Do you board animals?' And they gave their phone number."

"Wow," Alex said, sitting up. "That's the second request for pet-sitting. You might have stumbled onto a good summer job! How much will they pay?"

"I don't know. And they didn't say what kind of animal either."

"Call them!"

Morgan hesitated only a moment. If she rescued those animals at the shelter, she'd have a lot more pets to feed than she did now. Money for boarding two animals would help, and both pets would be gone before Mom and Maya returned home. "I'll call."

She used the phone in Maya's room, said very little, then hung up. She turned toward Alex. "You won't believe this one."

"Worse than the glamorous guinea pig?"

"I don't know." She paused. "The pet they want me to baby-sit is a lawn mower."

chapter.8

Morgan laughed at Alex's stunned expression.

"Someone wants you to baby-sit a lawn mower?"

Morgan nodded, eyes wide. "That's what the man said. Her name is Madeline, and she's a goat."

Arms outstretched, Alex fell backward onto the bed. "I don't believe it!"

"It's a pet goat, I swear. He said it wouldn't cost anything to feed. If I moved it from tree to tree, it would mow my grass."

"Like you don't think your dad will notice a goat tied to your trees?"

"I'm not a total idiot," Morgan said. "I'll tie up the goat behind the barn. There are plenty of trees—and grass—back there."

After Alex left for the pool, Morgan waited on her front steps for the Bill Turner family to arrive. A station wagon soon pulled into her driveway. A boy and girl crawled out of the backseat. A goat bounded after them.

"Hi! I'm Bill Turner," said the man emerging from the driver's seat. "These are my kids, Cindy and Jason."

"We're going backpacking!" Jason said. "And camping in tents!"

Little Cindy nodded. "Madeline eats poison ivy, but it won't hurt her."

"Uh, that's nice," Morgan said, backing away when the goat nibbled on her T-shirt. "I don't think we have any though."

"My children raised Madeline from a baby," Mr. Turner said. "She's two now, and a beloved member of the family."

"Where's your barn?" Jason asked. "You don't have a barn."

"Yes, it's out back. Do you want to see it?" She hoped the kids would lead the overly friendly goat back there for her. She needed to get the goat out of sight of the neighbors. Right now it was hidden by the station wagon, but what if someone drove by?

"I'm more concerned with your grass supply and the shade," Mr. Turner said. "But let's make it quick. We've got a list of errands a mile long, then we need to pack."

"Sure. Come this way." Morgan led them around the side of the garage and pointed. "See that row of oaks? See the barn just through there?"

Mr. Turner squinted as he stared across the yard. "Yes. You have plenty of trees and grass too. Good. You won't have to mow *this* week!" He shook Morgan's hand. "The kids were sure excited to find your Web site. We've had absolutely no luck finding anyone who would take Madeline for a week."

Morgan eyed the goat with suspicion. She stood placidly between the children, eyeing her right back. "I'm sure Madeline and I will get along just fine. You have a good vacation."

She took the goat's lead rope and waited till the Turner family pulled out of the driveway. "Okay, Madeline, it's just you and me. Let's go." Morgan walked two steps before she was jerked to a stop. She looked back. Madeline had her hooves firmly planted as she stared at the disappearing station wagon.

"Hey, don't worry. They're coming back." Morgan tugged twice, and finally Madeline trotted along behind her. Navigating her through the backyard challenged Morgan to the max. First the goat stopped to nibble petunias, then she snatched at a bush and came away with a mouthful of twigs. "Stop that!" Morgan said, yanking her back. Ten minutes later she had her tied to a tree behind the barn with a longer rope she'd found. "Have fun!" she said, patting the goat's head. Madeline butted Morgan's leg. Morgan winced. That goat had a head like a rock.

Back in the barn she checked on Glamour Boy, who was actually snoring in his cage. *Good,* Morgan thought. One less thing to worry about.

She glanced at her watch. Oh, man, it was after three already! Not that she cared if she missed chatting with Maya, but she needed to make sure no one spilled her secret about the Pet Place. Not yet. Not till she had a chance to do what she needed to do.

Rushing to the house, she squelched the guilty feelings that continued to surface. She knew she was doing all this behind her parents' backs, but surely they would understand if they knew the circumstances. Hopefully, they'd never need to find out.

When she logged on, Maya and Bren were the only girls there. Morgan refreshed her chat screen to read their conversation. Mostly Maya was complaining about how hard she'd worked and how her back hurt and how her hands were chapped from scrubbing a million dirty windows.

nycbutterfly: one guy in a plaid suit wanted to turn the house into a funeral home!!!!

jellybean: who R U talking about?

nycbutterfly: the child arrives! where is every1?

jellybean: Amber & Jamie R working. Alex @ pool. what's the emergency?

nycbutterfly: what emergency?

jellybean: U said U R desperate about something!

nycbutterfly: dying of boredom IS desperate

jellybean: big whoop

chicChick: I can't believe anyone still wears a plaid suit. GROSS

jellybean: who? what suit?

nycbutterfly: the real estate lady brings people 2 look @ aunt's house. it's huge and ancient. 1 neat lady wanted 2 turn it into a tea room. and 1 said she'd make it a bed & breakfast. But this plaid suit guy--who was BALD and only about 30!!!--wanted it 4 a funeral home. UGH

chicChick: r u getting 2 the malls at all?

nycbutterfly: nada. but I jog every morning.

jellybean: U???? jogging??? like you mean, sweating?

nycbutterfly: shut up. U know I like 2 stay fit.

jellybean: ha!! U exercise in front of 2 fans in air conditioning

nycbutterfly: it just so happens that Rose jogs and I go with her

chicChick: U R kidding!

jellybean: that old lady jogs?

nycbutterfly: i'm not kidding. she's kinda cool. she said it helps her spirits. she refuses to get depressed. mom says Aunt Edith was a sour old woman 2 take care of

Morgan leaned back and shook her head in wonder. Great-aunt Rose jogged? And Maya jogged with her? She couldn't even picture it! The Maya *she* knew wouldn't be caught dead in public like that.

She continued to read their conversation for a while, but it consisted of Bren's shopping trip and who was at the pool the day before. Morgan couldn't have cared less. But she *did* need to make sure they weren't coming home any earlier.

jellybean: gotta go. told dad I'd work supper shift. when
     U coming home?
nycbutterfly: how quaint. she misses me!
jellybean: I miss the laptop.
nycbutterfly: cruel. mom said a week probably.
jellybean: ok. C ya

After changing for work, Morgan ran outside to make sure
Madeline was behaving like a good goat. Morgan peered around
the corner of the barn, hoping the goat wouldn't see her or want
to play. She didn't have time. With her face close to the warm
barn boards, Morgan peeked.

And groaned.

Madeline had already munched her way around the woodpile and weeds that grew up among some rusty machinery. Her
fur was grimy with dust and cobwebs and smeared with rust, but
she seemed content. Luckily the Turner family couldn't see their
"beloved member of the family" just now. Morgan made a mental note to brush the goat sometime after work and sighed. It
must be ninety degrees in the shade. Should she get a fan and a
long extension cord rigged up somehow? The last thing she
wanted to brush later was a sweaty goat.

At the Gnosh, she forgot all about her animals for the next two
hours. "Sorry about the mess," Amber said. "We've been busy all
afternoon. A tour bus came through."

Morgan sighed, tied on an apron, and got to work. Dirty booths and tables waited. She bused tables and ran loads in the dishwasher as fast as she could. She was careful to separate the meat from the leftover food. She dumped it in a big kettle with a lid.

"I've got more for you," Jamie whispered, keeping one eye on Benny. "In that plastic bucket at the back of the refrigerator."

Morgan gave her a thumbs-up sign, then headed back out to the tables. She'd just finished wiping the last booth when she caught a movement out of the corner of her eye. Her dad had emerged from his office and was waving her over.

She grabbed her dishrag, then joined him. "What's up?"

"Your mother just called," he said, "with some surprising news."

Morgan's heart nearly stopped. They were coming home early! "Wha—uh, what did they say?"

"They found a buyer for Edith's house—someone making a bed-and-breakfast—and instead of moving Rose to an apartment, they're bringing her home. She doesn't have any relatives in Johnston anymore."

"Great-aunt Rose is going to live with us?" Morgan's eyes opened wide. "Where will we put her?"

"Not *with* us," her dad explained, "although she might stay a few days till they find her a place of her own. Get this. The plan was Maya's idea!"

Morgan scratched her head. "Maya's idea?"

"That's what your mom claimed."

"Well, what do you know?" Morgan linked her arm through

her dad's and walked back to the office with him. "Actually I have a bigger shock for you. Prepare yourself. Every morning Maya and Aunt Rose go *jogging*. Together. In *public*."

"No!"

"Maya said so in the chat room. Said Rose wears a pink jogging suit."

Her dad laughed and shook his head. "Now I'm really looking forward to meeting this lady."

Morgan hesitated. "Did they say for sure when they'd be home?"

"Not for sure, but it will be at least next Thursday, I imagine. Maybe Friday."

Morgan nodded. A week yet. That would be enough time. Barely enough.

She went to help Amber and Jamie scour the kitchen after the last customers paid and left. Her dad had errands to run. "Can you take me home?" Morgan asked Amber.

"Sure. Don't you want to wait for your dad? He'll be back soon."

"Not tonight. I've got a huge plastic bucket of leftovers to sneak out." Morgan figured that the more free food she salvaged from the Gnosh, the more allowance money she'd have to help the shelter animals.

Amber frowned. "Morg, when are you going to tell your dad about this? From the sound of things, you're getting in deeper."

"Not really. The goat and guinea pig will only be there a week, and I'm just boarding them to pay for food."

Amber cocked her head to one side. "What was all that I heard you telling Jamie earlier? You know. About rescuing animals from that shelter?"

Morgan stared at the floor, still wet from being mopped. "I wish I could. Alex overheard the owner say they were bankrupt. They're sending all the animals to the county pound on Monday." Morgan took a deep breath. "If they don't find homes fast, they'll be put to sleep. I'd die if that happened."

Amber said nothing, then finally grabbed the plastic bucket of leftovers. "Come on. Let's get you home." She didn't say another word till she pulled into the Crosses' driveway. "Morg, please pray about this. God will help you! I believe your dad would too. You don't have to carry this load by yourself."

"I know. I saw your verses at the Web site."

Amber grinned. "Was I that obvious?"

"Yeah."

Amber tapped a light rhythm on the steering wheel. "I don't know how much longer I can keep your secret. It's lying to your dad, and I feel guilty."

"I do too." Morgan got out. "I'll tell him soon. I promise."

But when? Morgan slipped around the side of the house and headed to the barn. She'd get the animals fed and watered before her dad got home, then take a shower and fall into bed. She was beat.

In the barn, she switched on the weak overhead light. The shadows outside its range were deep and dark. In years past it had petrified Morgan to be out there alone, but somehow, with the animals, it seemed a friendly and safe place.

The collie and kittens attacked the leftovers eagerly. Morgan slouched in her old red wagon and checked the guinea pig, then went to get Madeline. Although it was plenty warm, Morgan didn't feel right about leaving her out all night. The shadows were more gray than black behind the barn, and once her eyes adjusted, she spotted the goat. For some reason, Madeline had her nose down in the woodpile. What had she found there?

When Madeline turned toward Morgan, she emitted a weak bleat. Then a louder bleat. It sounded like she was crying!

"What's the matter?" Morgan said, hurrying to the woodpile.

When she knelt down, she spotted the problem. Madeline hadn't trapped some critter in the woodpile. She was tangled up so badly, with the rope caught and twisted in the stack of logs, that she could no longer move. Her fur was matted and dirty, and from the looks of the worn hair at her collar, she'd been jerking hard for hours to get loose. "I'm so sorry!" Morgan said over and over. She was lucky Madeline hadn't choked herself to death.

Morgan tried to untangle her but couldn't see well enough. She'd have to unhook the rope from the goat's collar. Madeline bleated and cried when she left to get another short rope but nuzzled her hand and drooled on her when she returned. Morgan grimaced and wiped her hands on her shorts. "I know you're grateful, but please don't slobber on me. And stand still!"

After snapping the new rope onto Madeline's collar, Morgan

unhooked the tangled one and left it dangling from the wood-pile. She'd untangle it tomorrow when she could see better. No one would notice it there anyway.

She put Madeline in the second horse stall on the other side of the collie. Sawdust and old hay covered the floor, and Madeline soon made herself a soft bed. Morgan was so tired she could have lain down right beside her and fallen asleep.

That night she waited up to have a bowl of Rocky Road ice cream with her dad, but he wasn't hungry, was too tired to talk, and just wanted to watch the news. Sighing, Morgan dragged herself off to bed.

However, long after she heard her dad go to bed, she was still staring, wide-eyed, at the dark ceiling. After what Amber said, she felt even guiltier for hiding the cats. Yet she was worried sick about the shelter animals. Somehow she'd have to find a way to liberate them without the Harts knowing she was the guilty party. Maybe she should have forged her dad's signature on the permission papers after all, Morgan thought. Yet somehow that seemed worse than rescuing the animals on her own and taking responsibility for it.

Would that be stealing? Her heart pounded at the thought. No, how could it be? She was saving lives. She was actually setting them free. She'd call it Operation Freedom! It was like rescuing prisoners of war who would go to an almost certain death if she didn't *do* something. How could that be wrong? Morgan rolled over and pounded her pillow. How could she ever live with herself if she ignored the animals' very real danger?

She tossed back and forth. She stared up into the dark. As she lay there, a breakout plan slowly formed in her mind. It would be risky, and she'd need some help, but as she considered it from all angles, the conviction grew that she could do it.

She was still wide awake when her bedside clock read 1:00 A.M., so Morgan decided to check her e-mail. Maybe people wanting pets had finally found her site.

Sneaking down the dark hall to Maya's room, she quietly closed the bedroom door and turned on the desk lamp. She wiggled the computer mouse and watched the screen come into view. The beeps and squawks of dialing up the Internet sounded so loud in the silent house. Finally, though, she could check her e-mail.

Six messages, and not one Sender name she recognized. She opened them eagerly, reading one inquiry after another about the Pet Place. One family wanted hamsters, one boy wanted a python (*Oh, right!* Morgan thought), one lady wanted to sell Morgan a horse, and one first-grade girl wanted a talking bird. Morgan's hopes deflated as she read. An older man had broken his leg and needed his dog walked every day, and the last e-mail was from a family needing a baby-sitter for their pregnant dog while they took a trip.

Morgan pounded her fist on her leg. Not a single good adoption contact! She didn't want more animals to baby-sit. She shook her head. Birds. Hamsters. Snakes. Didn't anyone want kittens anymore?

If only she could talk this over with her dad! If he hadn't been gone such long hours the last few days, she might have found the courage to confide in him. Maybe . . . Maybe she'd catch him at breakfast if she got up early. If she could just find a way to make him understand.

Crawling back into bed, Morgan barely touched her pillow before falling asleep. Her dreams were full of Madeline. In the first nightmare Madeline ate Glamour Boy in one big gulp. Next Madeline kicked all the windows out of her mom's van. In the final panicky dream Madeline gave birth to eight baby goats; Morgan thrashed about, frantically trying to corner the babies before they destroyed the entire Cross house. Morgan awakened early Friday morning, her covers twisted in knots.

She dragged herself downstairs, her "confession" speech prepared, but her dad only grabbed a banana on the way out the door. "I told Benny I'd stop at that fruit market and buy fresh melons this morning. I'd better run." He turned and squeezed Morgan's shoulders and kissed the top of her head. "I'm sorry for the rush, Jellybean. I really am. Your mom will be home in a few days, and everything will get back to normal."

"It's okay," Morgan said.

As soon as he pulled out of the driveway, Morgan called Alex. She waited while Grandma McGee got Alex out of bed.

"You have to help me today!" Morgan cried when Alex made it to the phone.

"Do you know what time it is?" Alex snarled. "What's going on?"

"I need help. Can you come over right away?"

"No! I'd need toothpicks to keep my eyes open!"

"Please come. *Please.*"

"This had better be important."

"Life and death," Morgan assured her.

Morgan had tied Madeline to a tree where she could munch on grass when Alex arrived.

"How's the dust mop?" she asked. Morgan was sitting at the picnic table brushing Glamour Boy's fur.

"Snobby. Always has his nose in the air." She set him down in his cage and closed the lid.

"Probably trying to breathe through all that hair!"

Morgan giggled, grabbed the carrier, and set off for the barn. Alex fell in step beside her. "So what's so important that you stole my beauty sleep?" she asked.

"Last night I realized what I have to do to save the animals at the shelter."

"Why do *you* have to do *anything?*"

"I could never forgive myself if I didn't. I need your help to move the animals from the shelter to my barn. Then I'll use the Web site to find homes for them all."

"You mean what I think you mean?"

"Yes." Morgan squared her shoulders. "We have to break them out at night after the Harts go home."

"Are you crazy? I'm not doing that!"

Morgan stopped and faced Alex, near tears. "Can't you *please* help me? I can't do it alone!"

"This is the worst goody-two-shoes thing you've tried yet!" Alex snapped. "Can't you just relax and have fun this summer like a normal kid?"

"Can *you* relax knowing all those animals could be *dead* in just a few weeks?"

"Yup. No problem at all."

"I don't believe you! Anyway, I can't, and I'm begging you to help me."

Before Alex could answer, a deafening *crash* made Morgan jump. She dropped the carrier so abruptly that Glamour Boy squealed, honked, and whirled around in circles.

"What was that?" Alex asked.

"I don't know. It came from the other side of the trees." Morgan knelt and reached inside the carrier to stroke the frantic guinea pig. "Shhh! There now." She patted what she hoped was the hairy animal's head. "At least I know it's not Madeline. I tied her up to the cherry—" Morgan glanced over her shoulder. "Oh, no!"

The *rope* was still attached to the tree trunk, but Madeline was nowhere in sight.

"Where'd she go?" Morgan cried.

More thunderous racket made Morgan and Alex break into a run. There was no sign of Madeline in the weeds near the woodpile or behind the barn. Bleating and the tinkle of breaking glass, however, pointed Morgan in the right direction.

"The playhouse!"

Morgan's heart sank as they ran to the empty playhouse on the other side of the barn. Just a few days ago Morgan had peeked in, remembering the fun she'd had there with Maya as a little girl. There was still a cot, some books, and toys in there. She arrived, panting, at the door of the playhouse. It was always closed. Now it stood wide open.

"Madeline!"

Morgan halted in the doorway in horror, watching a disaster unfold right before her very eyes.

"Stop!"

Morgan stepped into her playhouse, then jumped back as Madeline leaped over her from the cot to the little table. The frantic goat whipped around, knocking over the table and two chairs, then bounded from the cot to the floor, and back onto the cot. Arms up to cover her face, Morgan tried to get close, yet stay clear of the flying hooves.

Alex erupted into peals of laughter.

"Knock it off and help me!" Morgan cried.

"Sorry!"

Alex inched into the playhouse while Morgan whispered in what she hoped were soothing goat sounds. Madeline answered in frenzied bleats.

Finally, after circling the cot with smooth, gliding steps, Morgan and Alex cornered Madeline. Morgan grabbed the goat's collar and pulled her off the cot and outside. Then she quickly surveyed the damage. Torn books, a muddy doll, and broken furniture were strewn from one side of the playhouse to the other. Morgan closed her eyes and leaned against the door frame, suddenly dizzy from the heat.

"How'd she open the door?"

Morgan shook her head. "I looked in here a few days ago. I guess I didn't latch it tight. She just butted it open with her cement head." Morgan turned from the depressing sight. "I'll clean it up after I re-stake her. Can you stick Glamour Boy in the barn before he croaks from a heat stroke?"

"Sure." Still grinning, Alex went to get the honking guinea pig. Keeping one hand in a firm grip on the goat, Morgan dragged her behind the barn and tied her to a tree far from the woodpile, then returned to the playhouse.

Heat radiated from Morgan's face as she and Alex cleaned the playhouse. Madeline had smashed a glass jelly jar that Morgan had once used as a vase for bouquets of dandelions and violets. A pink ceramic cat Morgan had made in third grade had lost its head and tail in the fray. Alex swept the floor, then stripped the muddy pillow case and blanket off the cot.

With a sigh, Morgan finally closed the playhouse door and trudged back to the house with the filthy bedding. "Let me throw this in the washer, then I'll meet you out front."

"Okay, but understand something. This is the *last* time I'm volunteering at that shelter."

"I know, but you're not really volunteering today. You're spying for Operation Freedom." Morgan was back in five minutes and hopped on her bike. "Keep your eyes open. We have to decide which cages to take and how to get them home."

"You'd better pump Lover Boy for some information too."

"Lover Boy?"

"Oh, come on. Don't pretend you don't notice how Tiny Todd follows you around! I didn't see him offering to help *me* the other day, and I could have really used it!"

Morgan blushed. Some girls might think Todd wasn't much to look at, but he was awfully nice. She especially liked how much he loved the animals.

"Morg, are you listening?"

"Right. Pump him for what?"

"Find out what schedule they keep on Sundays. When they feed animals, walk dogs, stuff like that. We can't have them show up when we're snatching the animals."

When they arrived at the Have-a-Hart shelter, they parked their bikes at the side of the building. "The things I do for you," Alex muttered.

"Would you please stop saying that?" Morgan sputtered. "I do stuff for you too."

"Sorry." Alex grinned. "You've saved my Texas hide more than once."

"Yeah. And don't you forget it."

They entered the shelter together, but as usual no one was up front. "This is great," Alex whispered. "You go on back and tell them we're here to work. Keep them busy for a while. I'll snoop around the desk."

"Stay off her computer though. Don't break anything."

"Just go!"

Morgan looked dubious but disappeared through the rear door into the main part of the shelter. Barking dogs and meowing cats created such a din that she felt like covering her ears. Must be feeding time. Either that, or the poor animals were starving and howling for food. That was a definite possibility. Morgan remembered how bare the storage room shelves had been.

"Hello?" she called. "Hello?"

She waited. Apparently they couldn't hear her over the animal noise. Maybe they were outside. She peered into the storeroom as she passed. Empty. Glancing over her shoulder first, Morgan slipped inside the small room and checked the window. It was up maybe three inches. Guilt washed over her as she pushed the window up all the way. Thankfully, there was no screen. With any luck at all, the Harts would forget to shut the window and leave them an easy way in—and out with the animals.

Back in the hall, she headed toward the dog pens. Todd and his mom must be back there, cleaning kennels or exercising animals. But before she went another ten feet, a hissing sound behind her made her jump.

"*Pssssst!*"

Morgan turned. Alex was clear at the other end of the hall, waving wildly at her. What in the world? Morgan trotted back to where Alex waited at the lobby door. "What's up?"

"Let's get out of here."

"Wait! I never found Todd. I don't know their Sunday schedule yet."

"Doesn't matter. Come on." Alex grabbed her arm and pulled her through the lobby door, then on outside.

"Alex! What's going on?"

Around the corner, out of sight of the front door and windows, Alex turned. "Their Sunday schedule doesn't matter. I saw a note by the phone. The county pound is sending a truck tomorrow to pick up the animals." She paused. "They're coming at noon tomorrow."

chapter.9

They're going to the pound tomorrow?" On Saturday?" Morgan grabbed Alex's arm. "You're sure?"

Alex nodded. "So what's Plan B?"

"We do it tonight! Come on." They discussed the new plan on the way home. At the corner where they usually parted, they stood on the sidewalk for another twenty minutes, nailing down the details. Finally Morgan climbed on her bike. "See you tonight. Eight sharp. Don't be late. *And don't tell anyone.*"

Alex made a zipping motion across her lips, then pedaled toward home. Morgan's heart raced at the thought of Operation Freedom. If only there were another way. If only she could tell her dad. But she didn't dare. They couldn't breathe a word to anyone.

That night at eight, Alex arrived with her backpack. "All set?" she asked when Morgan answered the door.

"Yup. Dad knows you're spending the night. He's working till almost eleven, he said. Thankfully the Gnosh's open late tonight. He's doing books after they close."

"Got the wagon and ropes and everything?"

"Behind the house. I just wish we had more than one wagon. It's going to take a lot of trips to get all the cages."

"We can't get all the cages, but we can get lots of them. We can stuff several animals in each cage too. I'll pull the wagon."

"Okay, then I'll take the dogs, two at a time. I figure I'll tie one to each of my handlebars to keep them apart. If I go slow, they can keep up."

"I'll be slow anyway with that wagon." Alex dumped her backpack in the kitchen. "Let's go."

"Wait. Chat room first."

"The chat room? Are you nuts?"

"Listen! Jamie and Amber know you're staying overnight with me. If we don't get on, Maya might get suspicious and tell Mom. I don't want her calling when we're gone."

"Oh. Okay."

Morgan turned on the computer in Maya's room, then clicked over to TodaysGirls.com. Amber's Thought for the Day was from Psalm 104:14, 21.

"You make the grass for cattle. . . . The lions roar as they attack. They look to God for food." God has been caring for the animals since before he made humans! He won't stop now.

Alex pointed. "She's a little obvious, isn't she?"

"Kinda. She really wants me to tell Dad about everything. And I will! When the time is right. He's just got bigger things on his mind right now." Morgan opened the chat room screen.

nycbutterfly: Aunt Rose found a buyer for this haunted house finally.

jellybean: dad already told me today

nycbutterfly: I can tell the others, can't I?

jellybean: sorry!

chicChick: WHEN r u coming home? I haven't had a good trip to the mall since you left. UR missing sum GR8 sales!

nycbutterfly: early next week 4 sure. the people who bought the house 4 a bed & breakfast r buying lots of the furniture and junk. won't have 2 much 2 move

jellybean: i'm enjoying the peace & quiet here

rembrandt: isn't Alex staying w/ U 2nite?

jellybean: yeah. we're watching videos all night

nycbutterfly: U girls stay out of my room, u hear? Don't touch my clothes!!!!

jellybean: we get to use the computer in here. U took the laptop, remember?

nycbutterfly: my room better not B trashed!

jellybean: 2 L8. Alex tracked mud all over your carpet and slept in ur bed.

chicChick: like so gross!!!!!!!!

nycbutterfly: Morgan UR in BIG trouble!

jellybean: relax. just kidding.

nycbutterfly: U'd better be!

When the chat was over, Morgan checked her e-mail one more time. No new requests. With any luck, though, she could e-mail the family tomorrow who wanted hamsters and tell them to come get some. Ignoring the faintly nauseous feeling in her stomach, she turned to Alex.

"Let's go!"

After changing into black jeans and T-shirts and grabbing flashlights, they set off. Alex tied the wagon to her bike, and it sounded deafening as they bumped and banged over the back streets across town. With the sky overcast, it was dark earlier than usual. Morgan glanced at her watch as they passed under a streetlight: 8:45. Her heart raced. Even if her dad didn't come home till eleven, they had a lot of trips to make!

At the shelter, they rode their bikes around back, the wagon bump-bumping over the uneven ground. "Keep your fingers crossed," Morgan said. "If somebody closed the storeroom window, we're up a creek without a paddle."

But luck was with them. The window was up as high as she'd left it.

"Come on. Hurry." Alex knelt on one knee.

Morgan stuck her flashlight in her back pocket, looked over her shoulder to make sure they weren't being watched, then stepped up on Alex's bent knee. Bracing her hands on the window sill, she nearly shot through headfirst when Alex stood and gave her legs a boost.

"Alex! Careful!" Arms flailing, Morgan finally got a grip on the window frame and eased herself in through the window. "Don't let go of my legs yet."

With Alex firmly grasping her ankles, she lowered her body into the storeroom. As soon as her hands touched the floor, she said, "I'm in. Let go." She pulled her legs in after her and dropped to the dirty floor. She stood and peered out the window. "I'll meet you at the back door."

She pulled out her flashlight and flipped it on, pushing back the darkness of the storeroom, then moved out into the hall. As she swung her flashlight beam back and forth, four or five dogs woke up and started barking. "Shhh!" she said, hurrying down the hall to the back door. She unlocked it, and Alex slipped inside.

Alex aimed her light beam at the wall and grabbed two

leashes off a rack. "I'll get the two calmest dogs first. You get the cages. Four small ones or two of the bigger ones should fit, I think."

Hair stood up on the back of Morgan's neck as she made her way into the center part of the building. After adding two more hamsters to Cinnamon's cage, she piled the crowded mice cage on top. She carried them to the back door, then came back for the angora rabbit. Snowball's cage was big enough to hold three more kittens, but it would have to wait for the second trip. She left the rear door unlocked on her way out. They'd be back.

Outside, Alex tied the three cages and wooden box, stacked two on two, in the wagon, then wrapped a long rope around and around to anchor them. Morgan held both dogs' leashes till Alex finished, then they tied one of the dogs to each of Morgan's handlebars.

"Ready?" Alex asked, climbing on her bike.

"I think so." Morgan pedaled off, with a big black curly haired dog on one side and a golden Lab trotting along on the other side. Alex was right behind, the cages clunking together with every bump she hit.

Everything went fine for six blocks. Then they arrived at an intersection the same time as a car full of boys. Their stereo was loud enough to wake the dead. Both dogs barked, then bolted in opposite directions.

"Wait! Stop!" Morgan braced her legs against the pavement, but the dogs were too strong. Her bike toppled over. "Ow!" The golden Lab barked in her ear, while the black dog tried to drag them all down the street after the car.

"You okay?" Alex hopped off her bike and grabbed the black dog. "Here, let me have him."

"You already have the cages." Morgan noted the rip in her jeans. She could feel blood running down inside her pants leg. "Anyway, I'm fine." She winced when she stood.

Alex took the black dog anyway. "We're only two blocks from your house. Let's walk the rest of the way." She tied the black dog close to her own handlebars so the cages were out of reach, then started walking, pushing her bike.

Morgan limped behind, the Lab now trotting quietly along with her. As they passed under the next streetlight, she peered at her watch. "Alex, it's after 9:30! And this is only our first trip! What are we going to do?"

"Don't worry. I've got an idea." Alex refused to say what it was till they got the animals unloaded in the barn.

The three cages went in one empty horse stall, lined up side by side in the manger. Each of the dogs was put into his own horse stall, and Alex latched the doors securely. But the horrendous barking of all three dogs set the cats to yowling.

"You still have any leftovers?" Alex asked. "If you don't shut these dogs up, your neighbors will call the police."

Morgan raced for the house and grabbed the bucket from fridge. She had to get it out of there before her father saw it anyway. Back in the barn, they doled out meat scraps and bones to the three dogs, who immediately settled down to gnawing.

By then it was almost ten. Morgan was near tears. "We can't get any more of them out! There isn't time!"

"Not using our bikes." Alex paused. "But we could make at least two more trips if we used Maya's car."

"But we can't drive!"

"I can. My dad taught me in his truck. It was a stick, too, just like Mr. Beep."

Morgan nearly fainted at the idea. She knew where Maya kept her keys, but if she gave them to Alex, she was helping her drive without a license. But if she didn't, most of the animals at the shelter would be disposed of tomorrow! Which was more important? She decided quickly. "I'll get the keys."

Two minutes later they were backing out of the Crosses' driveway in Maya's Volkswagen. It died at the bottom of the drive. Alex muttered as she shifted. "Neutral, start, clutch, shift into first." She hit the gas and lurched forward a few feet, then the engine died. Morgan bit her lip. Alex started it again, revved the motor, shifted, then the Bug leaped forward several more feet before dying.

"I thought you could drive a stick!"

"I can! Give me a minute!" Alex pushed back her wild hair, took a deep breath, and started it again. "Clutch, shift, gas," she muttered. This time they leaped forward several feet and stopped, but the car didn't die. They crept forward again.

"We'd better not do this," Morgan said. "Turn around, Alex. We could go to jail!"

"Get some guts." Alex grinned. "I just needed to warm up."

Although the ride was anything but smooth, they did manage to cross town without killing the engine again. They drove around to the alley. Without a word, they hopped out and raced inside the shelter, flashlights on. Morgan got Snowball's cage, then added four more kittens from a second carrier. They hissed at each other, then quieted down. Outside, that carrier filled half the backseat.

Heart pounding, Morgan headed back indoors. Into a glass aquarium she dropped two gerbils, four fuzzy brown hamsters, and three white mice. She hoped they wouldn't eat each other before she got them home and separated again. Morgan wished she'd thought of combining cages before. They could have taken much more their first trip.

Balancing her flashlight on top of the aquarium, she hurried to the car and placed the aquarium on the floor of the backseat. Alex had already loaded a box of six cocker spaniel puppies and was trying to add a cage full of parakeets. The birds went crazy near the cats, squawking and flapping against the cage, so Morgan held the parakeets on her lap as they started back across town.

They had just reached the four-way-stop intersection at the corner when Morgan squealed, "Look! It's Todd!" Directly opposite them, under the streetlight, was a black car with an orange-and-yellow fireball on its side. Morgan ducked behind the birdcage.

Alex quickly turned sideways as Todd Hart's car came through the intersection toward them, then passed on by.

"He's going to the shelter!" Morgan said, turning to peer out the back window. "Did he see you?"

"No, it's too dark." Alex gave Mr. Beep some gas, jerked through the intersection, then headed home without further incident.

"We can't go back for any more!" Morgan wailed. "What about the others?"

Alex glanced at her sharply, but then her face softened. "You can't save the whole world, Morgan. You'll have your hands full as it is."

Morgan nodded miserably. Alex was right, but she felt like such a failure leaving some behind. When they added the new animals to the barn, they got pure pandemonium. "Don't you have some dog treats or something?" Alex asked.

"A few. I'll pass them out. Maybe some music would help again."

Alex started the CD player, and soon soothing music filled the barn. At first it had to be loud to be heard over the barking and hissing, but as things quieted down, she lowered the volume.

"It's after 10:30," Morgan said. "We have to be inside when Dad gets home. I just hope he didn't call while we were gone. I'll come back out after he goes to bed and make some bigger pens for the cats. I've got chicken wire left. They can't stay crowded in that carrier all night."

"I'll help. I didn't want to sleep tonight anyway."

They left the dim overhead light on but closed the barn door as they left. By the time Mr. Cross walked in the front door, Morgan and Alex were in pajamas and lying on the living room floor in front of a movie. Morgan felt such pangs of guilt. If her dad looked close, he'd know something was wrong.

But he barely spoke, other than to say he was exhausted and hoped that they'd had supper. "Mmmm," Morgan said, but her stomach growled. Now that he mentioned it, she didn't remember eating. "Want a sandwich or chips and dip?" she asked Alex. "I'm getting some."

"Sure." Alex followed her out to the kitchen when Mr. Cross headed upstairs. "I'm starving actually."

"Chow down then. We've got a long night ahead."

They waited until long after Mr. Cross called "good night" to them, then they put jeans on and headed back to the barn. It took over an hour to build two more pens from the chicken wire for the kittens and puppies. Morgan had brought all the pans she could find for water dishes and hoped the animals wouldn't chew on them. *That* would be hard to explain to her mom. It was nearly 2:00 A.M. when they dropped into bed.

Saturday morning they were still asleep when her dad left for work, but Morgan found the note he left on the kitchen table.

"'Saturday's busy,'" she read aloud. "'Come down and help when you get up. Hope you slept well. Love, Dad.'"

Morgan slumped at the table, then buried her tired head in her arms. "I can't go down and bus tables this morning." Her voice came out muffled. "I've got the animals to feed and water and exercise. Ms. Engles is picking up Glamour Boy this morning too. I can't wait to get that money."

"When's Madeline leaving?"

"Not till Monday."

Alex pushed an English muffin down in the toaster, then turned. "Before you beg me, yes, I'll bus tables for you. I'll tell your dad you weren't feeling so hot when you woke up."

Morgan examined her bruised, scraped knee and flexed her sprained wrist and shoulder. That, at least, was the total truth. "I'll come down just as soon as I can. You're a lifesaver."

"I know." Alex took a bow. "No applause. Just throw money."

"I would if I had any!"

chapter.10

After Alex left for the Gnosh, Morgan hobbled to the barn, trying to work the stiffness out of her leg and shoulders. She was glad it had rained in the night and cooled things off. At least it wasn't so humid this morning. She'd feed the animals inside, then go re-stake Madeline. She'd probably eaten every blade of grass she could reach behind the barn.

Inside, the cats meowed and dogs barked wildly when they saw her. With the upper hayloft doors open to catch the breeze, it was surprisingly cool in there too. She checked the animals in the wire cages in the manger. All was well.

Morgan frowned and blinked when dusty bits of straw filtered down through the air to land on her arms and Rex's cage. That was odd. She glanced overhead. What was up in the loft? Rats? Or were there more strays that she didn't know about staying in the barn?

Boards were nailed horizontally to the wall of the barn to form a ladder, and Morgan decided to climb up and check things out. She hadn't been in the loft in years. At the top she peered into the dimness but didn't see anything. Maybe it was mice. *Ugh.* She liked her mice in cages, thank you very much. Just then Morgan heard scraping noises below her, like something being pushed around. Morgan glanced down.

"Madeline!"

Morgan climbed down the board ladder, adding splinters to her sore hands. Madeline, head bent low, was chewing on an empty milk carton. The goat's rope trailed behind her, with the muddy stake she'd pulled loose still tied to the other end. Morgan rushed over and grabbed the goat's collar.

"You goofy goat! Where did you get this?" Morgan tossed the milk carton aside.

Madeline jerked back, but Morgan braced herself against the manger. Step by step, Morgan dragged Madeline across the horse stall and out the barn door, muttering under her breath all the while. Near the evergreens she tied Madeline's rope with a square knot to the axle of her dad's riding lawn mower.

"There! I dare you to drag *that* thing around."

Hurrying back to the house, Morgan ran another bucket of water from the outside spigot, pulling out splinters while waiting for the bucket to fill. Sighing, she shut off the water, grasped the bucket handle, and headed back to the barn. As she passed through the row of trees, she glanced sideways.

"Not again!"

She dropped the water bucket and ran. Madeline stood half on, half off, the riding lawn mower. Her front hooves were perched on top of the motor as she nibbled on the padded plastic seat.

Morgan grabbed the rope attached to Madeline's collar and jerked her down. "You're supposed to *be* the lawn mower, not *eat* it!" she cried. Pulling and tugging, she dragged Madeline around the barn to the trees behind. Even though she'd eaten the grass short there, she would have to make do for a while. "Now behave!" Morgan needed to feed and water all the animals, but she was starving herself. She strode back to the house for some breakfast, muttering, "I love all animals, I love all animals, I love all animals."

The phone was ringing when she walked into the kitchen. "Hello?"

"Is this Morgan Cross?"

"Yes, it is."

"This is Gloria."

Morgan drew a total blank. *Gloria who?*

"How's my Glamour Boy?"

"Oh! Ms. Engles! It's you. Where are you calling from?"

"From my house. I just got home. We had to sort through Mother's things, then deal with lawyers. I nearly lost my mind." She gave a wheezy sigh. Morgan shifted impatiently from one foot to the other. "I missed my Glamour Boy so much. He would have been such a comfort to me in my time of sorrow."

Morgan couldn't imagine that dust mop being a comfort to

anyone, but clearly Ms. Engles believed it. "Well, he got along fine while you were gone."

"Oh good. I can't wait another minute to see my sweet boy. I'll be right there to pick him up."

"Right now?" Morgan gulped. She'd planned to clean out Glamour Boy's cage that morning, then brush the guinea pig's silky hair till it shone. She wanted him to look his best so she got paid the full amount. "Can you come in an hour?"

"I couldn't possibly wait that long. I'll zip right out this minute. Toodle-oo." And she hung up.

Morgan closed her eyes and fought down the panic that rose inside her. She'd have to drop everything now and tend to Glamour Boy. She prayed for speed, then raced out to the barn. She had twenty minutes at the most before Ms. Engles arrived.

Grabbing an empty cardboard box, Morgan set the startled guinea pig into it. He whistled and honked in annoyance.

She brushed the hair off the quilted pillow, then set it and the toys to one side. With a rag, she wiped out the cage and polished the sides, wishing she had time to make it shine. She put fresh newspaper down then refilled the water bottle and food dish.

"Now for you, gorgeous."

She picked him up in the middle. With brush in hand, Morgan plopped down on a bale of straw and held a squealing Glamour Boy in her lap. Feeling ridiculous, she lifted chunks of his long hair to find which end of the short, plump body was the head.

"I should have let Alex mark the tail end," she muttered.

For several minutes, Morgan brushed and smoothed Glamour Boy's long hair. It had a sticky feel to it, but Morgan knew there was no time for the Strawberry Essence shampoo and conditioner. Shaking her head, she could just imagine the guinea pig with its hair set in curlers.

"Hold still!" She grabbed the warm guinea pig as he tried to scramble over the edge of her lap. "You have to stay clean." When Morgan heard a car pull into their driveway, she tossed Glamour Boy's brush into the embroidered bag that held his blanket and hooded sweatshirt.

Ms. Engels was thrilled to hold Glamour Boy again. After paying Morgan, she baby talked him all the way to her car, making little smoochy noises.

While Morgan was still finishing her breakfast, Alex knocked on the back door and let herself into the kitchen. "You're just now eating?"

"Been a long morning. Glamour Boy just went home. Madeline got loose again."

"Breakfast crowd was light," Alex said, pulling out a chair. "Amber and Jamie can handle lunch while your dad does the cash register. He sent me here to check on you, to see if you're *feeling better*."

Morgan rolled her eyes. That made her feel even guiltier. "Did you say I was sick?"

"Just queasy, like you ate something bad."

"Thanks for covering for me." She pushed her chair back and rubbed her sore leg. "I still haven't fed and watered anybody."

"Let's go then."

The next forty minutes whizzed by as they fed and watered the caged animals, playing with each animal except the mice. Moving to Cinnamon's cage, she stopped short and gasped. She couldn't believe her eyes.

The hamster was dead!

Fingers trembling, Morgan opened Cinnamon's cage. The hamster had been asleep in his exercise wheel only fifteen minutes earlier, curled up in a ball so tight that Morgan couldn't tell his nose from his rear end. Now he lay belly up, legs spraddled, on the newspaper-covered floor of the cage.

Morgan's hand shook as she reached into the cage and lifted the fat, fuzzy-looking animal. His chubby appearance was deceptive; half of it was long hair. Gently Morgan wiggled the hamster.

"Come on, Cinnamon, wake up. Don't be dead." She rolled him over into the palm of her other hand. "*Please* don't be dead."

As she held her breath, the fat lump of fur began to stir. Then, without warning, Cinnamon looked up, bared his teeth, and let out a piercing squeal. Morgan dropped him. He landed back in his cage.

"Sorry. Sorry!" *What a crab,* Morgan thought. Todd had been right.

Keeping a close eye on the grouchy hamster, Morgan filled

his food dish with a mixture of seeds, cereals, and dried vegetables to pack into his cheek pouches.

Alex finally covered the glass aquarium holding Salt, Pepper, and the other mice. "I'm done. What else?"

"That's all. Want to watch a movie or something?"

"Sure."

The phone was ringing when they got inside. Morgan grabbed it. "Hello?"

"Morgan, honey, it's Dad. Are you okay?"

Morgan ducked her head. "I'm fine now. Sorry I couldn't help this morning."

"That's okay. Is Alex there with you, by any chance?"

"Yeah, we're going to watch a movie."

"I have a big, *big* favor to ask you two. Jamie cut herself when slicing some bread—"

"Is she okay?"

"Yes, but I took her to get stitched up, then took her home."

"Stitches? How many?"

Alex pulled on Morgan's arm. "What happened?"

"Jamie got hurt," she said. "How many stitches?"

"I don't know for sure, but she can't work, and I could really use you girls. Pronto."

"We'll be right there."

"Thanks, Jellybean. Say, with all the excitement, I almost forgot," her dad said. "Your mom called earlier."

"How are things going with selling the house?"

"Much better than expected. In fact, she was calling from Freemont. They've already started home. Should be here about six-thirty."

Morgan's hand froze to the phone. *Six-thirty? Tonight?* Morgan jerked and dropped the phone.

chapter.11

The phone clattered on the kitchen floor. Morgan reached down to grab it.

"Morgan? You there?" her dad called.

"Sorry!" Her mind raced, trying to absorb the news. "So, um, they're all coming home tonight? Where's Aunt Rose going to live?"

"She's staying with us a week or so till they find an apartment she likes." He paused. "Well, I'd better get back to work. I'd like to close early tonight. See you girls in fifteen minutes?"

"Sure. We'll be there." Morgan hung up and shook her head. "Alex, what am I going to do when Mom and Maya get home? I'm going to be in so much trouble!"

"I warned you this could happen!"

"Thanks a lot! I don't need you to say *I told you so*."

"Sorry. Hey, maybe they won't find out about the animals till you find homes for everyone. You said yourself that nobody goes out there anymore. You can barely see the barn from the house with that row of trees."

"True." Morgan glanced at her watch. "I hate to ask you—I mean, you've already done so much today . . ."

"*Now* what?"

"Dad wanted us both to come to the Gnosh and help out. He'll pay you."

Alex rolled her eyes. "The things I do for you."

"I owe you."

"Big time."

Morgan and Alex were busy from the minute they stepped into the Gnosh till Mr. Cross said he was ready to leave at six o'clock.

"How can you?" Morgan asked, looking around the restaurant. Eight tables and booths were still full.

"Amber said not to worry. She'll close later after everyone leaves." He headed out the door. "Let's go! We don't want Mom and Maya to beat us home!"

Morgan looked at Alex and gulped. What he said was true, but her dad had no idea the real reason why.

But when they turned onto Jackson Street, Morgan's dad whistled. "Well, will you look at that!"

Morgan craned her neck to see around her dad. There, parked in their driveway, was Mom's van. An orange U-Haul trailer was hooked behind, and its back door stood open.

They pulled in next to the trailer, and soon Morgan's parents were hugging. Then her dad hugged the woman who had to be Aunt Rose. Morgan and Alex hung back until they were introduced. Aunt Rose, dressed in a bright green jogging suit, reached over and kissed Morgan's cheek. "You're the spittin' image of your mother," she said. "I'm so glad to finally meet you."

"Me too. Maya's told me a lot about you." Morgan glanced at the house. "Is she inside?"

"Probably already on the phone," Alex said.

"Actually, she's helping with Rose's things," her mom said. "There's no room in the garage, but we have to return the empty trailer tomorrow." She smiled at her husband. "We thought she could store her things in the barn for now."

Morgan choked, then coughed, then coughed some more. Alex pounded her on the back, but she kept coughing.

"Are you all right, honey?" her mom asked.

"Sure. Sorry." Morgan smiled faintly. "I don't know about the barn. It's probably pretty dirty."

"True, but most of this stuff's in boxes. The furniture's coming later. So that'll be okay." Mrs. Cross peered around the garage. "Now where's Maya?"

Morgan frowned. "Isn't she in the house?"

Her mom shook her head. "We needed something to cart Rose's things to the barn. I sent Maya down there to look for your old wagon."

Morgan stopped breathing. Alex grabbed her arm and gave her a gentle shove. "Let's go help her find it," she said, smiling at Mrs. Cross. "Come on, Morgan."

They hurried across the yard, but Morgan felt like her legs were going to buckle at any moment. Maya was in the barn! Her worst nightmare had come true already! "Oh dear Lord, please help me! I don't know what to do. Help!"

They arrived at the barn door and stepped inside. Maya stood in the center of the main room, turning slowly, a bewildered expression on her face. Cats meowed, dogs growled, hamsters ran on their squeaky wheels, and parakeets sang. As Maya completed her circle, she spotted Morgan and Alex in the doorway. "What is going on here?" she demanded. "Are you running a *real* funny farm?"

Morgan stepped into the barn. "More like Noah's ark. Remember how the animals went into the ark so they wouldn't die? Same idea here. I'm keeping the animals alive."

Maya spread her arms in both directions. "Wait till Mom sees this! I can't believe Dad let you do this the minute we left town."

"Wait! He didn't." Morgan swallowed hard. "Dad doesn't know about them."

"Oh sure! How could he possibly not know?"

"He's been at the Gnosh from sunup to really late all week."

Alex spoke for the first time then. "Most of these animals have only been here since last night."

"Morgan Cross," her sister said, "you'd better tell me right now what's going on, or I'm marching in the house and telling Mom and Dad."

"Please don't!" Morgan stood wringing her hands.

"Well?" Maya said.

Morgan sighed, then started with the day Maya left, telling about the shelter going bankrupt, putting up the pet adoption Web site, and ending with the daring rescue the night before. The only part she left out was how they'd used Mr. Beep.

"So please don't tell Mom and Dad, okay? Not yet. Let me do it when the time is right."

Maya knelt down and picked up a cocker spaniel puppy, holding it close to her face. It wiggled, then reached over and licked her nose. Maya laughed and rubbed noses with the puppy. Morgan glanced at Alex. Maybe they had a chance.

"I'll keep your secret," Maya finally said, "but they'll find out as soon as Dad unloads the U-Haul and brings Rose's stuff down here. I'll tell them the three of us can unload the trailer later."

"I can't believe you're being this nice about it!" Morgan blurted out.

Her sister laughed. "I can't either. But the animals remind me of Aunt Rose, in a way. She's homeless right now, too, and doesn't feel needed or wanted anywhere either." She gently set the puppy back in its pen. "I'd better get back with this wagon before they come looking for me."

Morgan and Alex followed Maya and the wagon back to the house. Inside, Aunt Rose sat on the couch in their living room. She was holding the anniversary picture of her sister, Edith, and her husband, Walter—the one Mrs. Cross had found in an album before they'd left. "Edie was always such a good sister," Rose said. "So generous with me all these years."

"You were good to her too," Mrs. Cross said. "I don't know what she would have done without you taking care of her."

"It's good to be needed." Rose's shoulders drooped, and there was a catch in her voice. Suddenly she seemed drab and sad, despite her bright green jogging suit.

Mrs. Cross glanced up then and noticed the girls. "Did you find the wagon?"

"I put it in the garage. Morgan and Alex are going to help me unload stuff later."

Aunt Rose looked up then. "I remember playing in that barn as a child."

"Really?" Maya sat down beside her.

"Oh yes! My brother Charles—your grandfather—helped our father build it all those years ago. We each had a pony, Charles and I, but Edith wouldn't ride. She was always too timid. And barn cats! We had a dozen cats at one time. Can you believe it? Oh, those were happy times." Her voice trailed off. "It's hard being the only one left who remembers."

Morgan glanced at Alex. Actually there were almost that many cats out there *now,* although her parents didn't know it.

Aunt Rose smiled wistfully. "At one time I had wanted to run a horse farm or even be a vet. I had a special way with animals. My grandma called it the gift."

"Must be where our Morgan gets her love for animals," Mr. Cross said. "She's always trying to save some endangered species. Just last week she rescued a litter of kittens from the Dumpster at work."

"Really?" Aunt Rose said. "I love kittens. Edith wouldn't permit cats in her house, but once I get my apartment, I'm getting a cat first thing." She smiled softly. "Sometimes you just need something to cuddle." Her voice trailed off, but the sadness in her eyes touched Morgan.

She glanced at Alex and could see Alex was thinking the same thing. There was someone in the barn that just might ease Aunt Rose's loneliness. That is, if Morgan was brave enough to go get him. Suddenly Morgan knew what she had to do. She had no idea what the consequences would be, and she was petrified to find out.

Taking a deep breath, she made up her mind. "I'll be right back," she said.

She ran across the backyard to the barn, picked Zorro out of the chicken-wire pen, then headed back to the house with him wrapped in her shirt. For a moment, she hung back in the living room doorway, then she entered. While everyone watched, she laid Zorro in Aunt Rose's lap. "He's a present for you."

"Why, Morgan, how sweet!" her mom said. Then she peered closer. "Isn't that one of the strays you were supposed to take to the shelter?"

Morgan gulped. "I did take them, but . . ."

"But what?" her dad asked.

"I brought them home again." Then in a tumbling rush of words, she told her parents everything she'd told Maya in the barn. Finally she ran out of breath. "I paid for the food by babysitting a goat and a guinea pig."

"I don't believe it!" her mom said. "And right under your father's nose!"

Her dad frowned. "You never took the animals to the shelter? You lied to me? And you stole animals last night from the shelter?" He glanced briefly at Alex then. "I don't believe it!"

Morgan fought the tears that welled up. "I'm really sorry about that," she said. "I didn't want to lie to you, but I just couldn't stand the idea of the animals going to that pound and getting put to sleep."

"I understand, but that's still no excuse, young lady."

"I know." She sighed. "Am I grounded?" Morgan saw her dad glance at her mom, eyebrows raised.

Finally he answered. "At least a month. And I mean only

going to the Gnosh for work. No pool. No Alex's. And I expect you to apologize to the Harts. Do you understand?"

Morgan glanced quickly at Alex, then looked away. "Yes."

"You girls could have been arrested for breaking and entering, not to mention stealing the animals." Mr. Cross shook his head, then finally put his arm around Morgan and squeezed her shoulders. "Why didn't you tell me what was going on?" he asked softly. "I could have helped you."

Morgan stared at the carpet, then glanced up. "You were so busy at the Gnosh. I didn't want to bother you when you had so much to handle this week."

"Don't you know by now that you're no bother?" her dad asked.

Morgan realized that that was what Amber had been trying to tell her all week. "I guess so."

Maya came and stood by Morgan. "Look at Aunt Rose," she whispered. The older lady held Zorro in her lap, rubbing the kitten's stomach as he lay on his back, purring. "She hasn't looked that happy since I met her."

Just then, Aunt Rose glanced up at Morgan. "Did you say you saved a whole barn full of animals? And why is the shelter closing?"

"The widow who runs it just doesn't have the funds to keep it open anymore. It's too bad too. Mrs. Hart is really nice."

Rose grinned first at Maya, then at Mrs. Cross.

"Rose, what are you thinking?" Morgan's mom asked.

"That Edith left me half her estate to donate to a worthy cause." Her eyes shone. "Keeping the shelter open might just be a good way to spend some of the money."

Morgan gasped. "Really? That'd be so cool!" She glanced at Alex, who was staring wide-eyed at Aunt Rose.

"On one condition," Aunt Rose said. "If I liked Mrs. Hart— was that her name?—I'd want to be half owner in the place."

"Now, wait a minute, Rose! You have to think about this," Mr. Cross said.

"Rose, don't rush into anything!" Mrs. Cross added. "That's too sudden!"

"Don't worry. I'm just thinking out loud." She laughed. "Like I said, I'd check it out first, show the accounts to a lawyer, look at the facilities." She smacked her lips and her dentures clicked. "But who knows? I may have just found my new lease on life!"

"But consider your age," Mrs. Cross said. "Now's the time for you to take it easy."

"There's time enough for that after I'm dead! I'm only sixty-two. Anyway, I wouldn't have to work any more hours than I wanted to."

Morgan could hardly contain herself. Her animals might be safe! Plus the ones she hadn't been able to rescue! She threw her arms around Maya, who pushed her away. "Get a grip, girl!"

"Sorry!" Morgan grinned at Alex, then knelt beside Aunt Rose and tickled Zorro under the chin. She couldn't believe it!

In just a few minutes, things had turned around in a way she could never have predicted. Aunt Rose could be the answer to her prayers!

And, Morgan suspected as she watched the older lady, these animals were the answer for Rose. *Thank you, Lord. Oh, thank you. I'm so sorry I didn't pray for your help or trust you sooner.*

She wished she had. Amber had been right about God caring about the details in her life, the things that mattered to her, including the homeless animals. She glanced up at her dad, who grinned down at her. He obviously cared about her too. She should never have doubted that. Next time she needed him, Morgan decided, she wouldn't hesitate to go to him.

chapter.12

That night, Morgan logged on to TodaysGirls.com for their evening chat. She couldn't believe so much had happened in the twenty-four hours since her Aunt Rose had arrived.

> nycbutterfly: greetings from my own bedroom! so good 2 B home!
>
> jellybean: greetings from Noah's ark. the cat's out of the bag
>
> TX2step: greetings from prison you mean!
>
> rembrandt: what happened when your parents found out?
>
> TX2step: Morgan got us both grounded 4 the rest of the summer!

jellybean: I didn't know dad would call ur grandpa. but it was worth it 2 me. get this! Aunt Rose may buy half of the animal shelter business and run it w/Lois Hart

nycbutterfly: it's going 2 B called Pet Partners when they have their grand re-opening!

jellybean: my web site is changing to www.PetPartners-Online.com & I get a commission on every pet I find a home 4

faithful1: do U need help changing the web site name?

jellybean: Maya said she'd do it. Rose saw the site and loved what U did

faithful1: i'm looking forward 2 meeting her

chicChick: is Rose living with U?

nycbutterfly: 4 a while. if she likes Mrs. Hart, she might rent a room from her. I guess she has this big house with lots of space

rembrandt: so all the animals U rescued are back there?

jellybean: we're taking them back tomorrow. all except Zorro. Aunt Rose is keeping him. what a crazy week!

TX2step: R summer is wiped out. Grandpa volunteered me 2 mow grass 4 like the whole neighborhood practically

nycbutterfly: u children are lucky Mrs. Hart likes Rose. taking the animals was illegal. U could have gotten arrested 4 that

TX2step: AND 4 driving Mr. Beep without a license.

nycbutterfly: what????????????? did U??????????????? my car???????

Morgan could hear Maya screaming in her bedroom. She exited the chat room, closed the computer, and was out the kitchen door and heading to the barn before Maya could run down the stairs. Morgan planned to hide in the hayloft. She could only count on so much sisterly love in one week.

And something told her she'd just used up her quota.

Net Ready, Set, Go!

I hope my words and thoughts please you.
Psalm 19:14

The characters of TodaysGirls.com chat online in the safest—and maybe most fun—of all chat rooms! They've created their own private Web site and room! Many Christian teen sites allow you to create your own private chat rooms, and there are other safe options.

Work with your parents to develop a list of safe, appropriate chat rooms. Earn Internet freedom by showing them you can make the right choices. *Honor your father and your mother (Deuteronomy 5:16).*

Before entering a chat room, you'll select a user name. Although you can use your real name, a nickname is safer. Most people choose one that says something about who they are, like Amber's name, faithful1. Don't be discouraged if the name you select is already taken. You can use a similar one by adding a number at its end.

No one will notice your grammar in a chat room. Don't worry if you spell something wrong or forget to capitalize. Some people even misspell words on purpose. You might see a sentence like How R U?

But sometimes it's important to be accurate. Web site and e-mail addresses must be exact. Pay close attention to whether letters are upper- or lowercase. Remember that Web site addresses don't use some punctuation marks, such as hyphens and apostrophes. (That's why the "Today's" in TodaysGirls.com has no apostrophe!) And instead of spaces between words, underlines are often used to_make_a_space. And sometimes words just run together like onebigword.

When you're in a chat room, remember real people are typing the words that appear on your screen. Treat them with the same respect you expect from them. Don't say anything you wouldn't want repeated in Sunday school. *Do for other people what you want them to do for you (Luke 6:31).*

Sometimes people say mean, hurtful things—things that make us angry. This can happen in chat rooms, too. In some chat rooms, you can highlight a rude person's name and click a button that says, "ignore," which will make his or her comments disappear from your screen. You always have the option to switch rooms or sign off. If a particular person becomes a continual problem, or if someone says something especially vicious, you should report this problem user to the chat service. *Ask God to bless those who say bad things to you. Pray for those who are cruel (Luke 6:28–29).*

Remember that Internet information is not always factual. Whether you're chatting or surfing Web sites, be skeptical about information and people. Not everything on the Internet is true. You don't have to be afraid of the Internet, but you should always be cautious. Practice caution with others even in Christian chat rooms.

It's OK to chat about your likes and dislikes, but *never* give out personal information. Do not tell anyone your name, phone number, address, or even the name of your school, team, church, or neighborhood. Be cautious. . . . *You will be like sheep among wolves. So be as smart as snakes. But also be like doves and do nothing wrong. Be careful of people (Matthew 10:16–17).*

AMBER THOMAS

N 2 DEEP & STRANGER ONLINE

16/junior
e-name: faithful1
best friend: Maya
site area: Thought for the Day

Confident. Caring. Swimmer. Single-handedly built
TodaysGirls.com Web site. Loves her folks.
Big brother Ryan drives her nuts! Great friend.
Got a problem? Go to Amber.

JAMIE CHANDLER

PLEASE REPLY! & PORTRAIT OF LIES

15/sophomore
e-name: rembrandt
best friend: Bren
site area: Artist's Corner

Quiet. Talented artist. Works at the Gnosh Pit after
school. Dad left when she was little. Helps her
mom with younger sisters Jordan and
Jessica. Baby-sits for Coach Short's kids.

ALEX DIAZ

4GIVE&4GET & TANGLED WEB

14/freshman
e-name: TX2step
best friend: Morgan
site area: Entertain Us

Spicy. Hot-tempered Texan. Lives with grandparents because
of parents' problems. Won state in freestyle swimming at her
old school. Snoops. Into everything. Breaks the rules.

OWER DRIVE & R U 4 REAL?
6/junior
-name: nycbutterfly
est friend: Amber
te area: What's Hot—What's Not

shion freak. Health nut. Grew up in New York City.
mall town drives her crazy. Loves to dance.
Dad owns the Gnosh Pit. Little sis Morgan is also
a TodaysGirl.

BREN MICKLER

UNPREDICTABLE & LUV@FIRST SITE
15/sophomore
e-name: chicChick
best friend: Jamie
site area: Smashin' Fashion

Funny. Popular. Outgoing. Spaz. Cheerleader.
Always late. Only child. Wealthy family. Bren is
chatting—about anything, online and off—
except when she's eating junk food.

MORGAN
CROSS

UN e-FARM & CHAT FREAK
4/freshman
-name: jellybean
est friend: Alex
ite area: Feeling All Write

he Web-ster. Spends too much time online. Overalls.
M&M's. Swim team. Tries to save the world. Close to her
amily—when her big sister isn't bossing her around.

Cyber Glossary

Bounced mail An e-mail that has been returned to its sender.

Chat A live conversation—typed or spoken through microphones—among individuals in a chat room.

Chat room A "place" on the Internet where individuals meet to "talk" with one another.

Crack To break a security code.

Download To receive information from a more powerful computer.

E-mail Electronic mail sent through the Internet.

E-mail address An Internet address where e-mail is received.

File Any document or image stored on a computer.

Floppy disk A small, thin plastic object that stores information to be accessed by a computer.

Hacker Someone who tries to gain unauthorized access to another computer or network of computers.

Header Text at the beginning of an e-mail that identifies the sender, subject matter, and the time at which it was sent.

Home page A Web site's first page.

Internet A worldwide electronic network that connects computers to each other.

Link Highlighted text or a graphic element that may be clicked with the mouse in order to "surf" to another Web site or page.

Log on/Log in To connect to a computer network.

Modem A device that enables computers to exchange information.

The Net The Internet.

Newbie A person who is learning or participating in something new.

Online To have Internet access. Can also mean to use the Internet.

Surf To move from page to page through links on the Web.

Upload To send information to a more powerful computer.

The Web The World Wide Web or WWW.